Praise for Deb
and her Jesus Creek mystery series

"Adams's books perfectly capture the rhythms of life in a small town, where everyone sees it as a God-given right to know everybody else's business."
—*The Baltimore Sun*

"This gentle, funny, suspenseful mystery series deserves a huge audience of devoted fans."
—NANCY PICKARD

"Compassionate, chilling, and compelling."
—GILLIAN ROBERTS

"Thoroughly enjoyable ... A mystery novelist to be reckoned with."
—*Nashville Banner*

"Adams captures both the intricacy and style of a well-crafted mystery, along with the comic elements of a truly Gothic Southern novel. In the process, she transcends both."
—STEVEN WOMACK

"Adams has a fluid, soft, and delightful writing style. . . . A terrific writer. My personal library contains all the 'All the' novels to date—and I'm leaving plenty of room for more to come."
—*The Nashville Tennessean*

By Deborah Adams
Published by Ballantine Books:

ALL THE GREAT PRETENDERS
ALL THE CRAZY WINTERS
ALL THE DARK DISGUISES
ALL THE HUNGRY MOTHERS
ALL THE DEADLY BELOVED
ALL THE BLOOD RELATIONS

ALL THE BLOOD RELATIONS

Deborah Adams

BALLANTINE BOOKS • NEW YORK

http://www.randomhouse.com

Library of Congress Catalog Card Number: 96-96976

ISBN 0-345-40378-9

Manufactured in the United States of America

First Edition: January 1997

10 9 8 7 6 5 4 3 2 1

This book is dedicated to Megan Bladen-Blinkoff, and to Millie, Ethel, and Rhoda, all of whom make morning coffee so much more fun.

WITH THANKS . . .

There's a vicious rumor that I am, well, overly
curious. This is not true, but it has caused a great
many people to stop taking my phone calls. Thank
goodness the following sensible souls were willing to
speak to me and answer numerous, sometimes
bizarre, questions while I was writing this book.

Jack Bonner and Ted Rice of Nature's Design
Florists allowed me to invade their sanctuary, and
they were generous with information, although far
more civilized than I would have liked.

Joe Blades and Joan Hess went out of their way
to provide me with material about UFO abductions.
I especially enjoyed their firsthand accounts of visiting the mothership.

D. J. Donaldson and Dr. Brannon Thomas helped
me research TLE. While I listened carefully and
tried my best to get it right, if there are any errors
of fact, I take full blame.

Dr. Dean James thoughtfully (and unwittingly)
provided a motivation that was so much better
than what I had planned, I had no choice but to
steal his idea.

Rhoni McCollum just kept putting me back on
that horse no matter how much I complained.

Agent John Meyer of the Tennessee Bureau of
Investigation provided me with an opportunity to do

a complete rewrite by giving me information about investigative procedure that did not fit the book I had planned. I suspect I'm in the computer now. Under *Psychopaths to watch out for.*

Jean Newsome, a veritable fountain of information, once again made my job much easier by answering a thousand questions. Of course, she has nothing else to do all day.

Jim O'dell started it all several years ago when, during a particularly dull time in his life, he devoted himself to the task of thinking up unusual murder weapons. It's taken a while, but I've finally managed to come up with the rest of his story.

Cast of Characters

Law Enforcement

Kay Martin: no longer the rookie cop on the Jesus Creek Police Department

Bernie: Kay's replacement; a rookie so green, if he was an apple, he'd give you a tummy ache

German Hunt: assistant police chief, newlywed, and good old boy

Al and Bill: daytime and nighttime dispatchers, respectively, and aren't we glad they don't patrol the streets?

Chief Reb Gassler: the poor fellow who puts up with the rest of them and escapes on his fishing vacations whenever possible

Special Agent Mark Warner of the Tennessee Bureau of Investigation: surely that explains it sufficiently

The Bradley Family

Marty Bradley: loving husband and father, owner of Bradley's Lumber Store, a thriving Jesus Creek business

Meredith Bradley: wife of Marty, mother of Bruce and Vanessa; successful florist

Bruce Bradley: Meredith's only son, Marty's only child, and husband of:

Trina Bradley: owner and namesake of Trina's Tea Room, the latest addition to downtown Jesus Creek

x   Cast of Characters

Vanessa Hyland: Meredith's daughter from a previous relationship

Townsfolk

Wayne Holland: Kay's significant other; a man who doesn't worry much about his girlfriend's lack of domestic skills because he is secure enough with his own masculinity to pick up after himself

Frankie Mae Weathers: outspoken, odd-dressing, bundle of energy despite her many years

Delia Cannon: one of the town's favorites; a woman seeking enlightenment

Roger Shelton: the Yankee with whom Delia consorts

Dr. Daryl James: replacement for the last Jesus Creek doctor, who, as some of you will recall, was not a particularly good role model for the town's youth

Mr. and Mrs. Veatch: easily the most fun couple in town

Eloise: owner of the local diner; reservoir of information

Scott Carter: a teenage boy who is headed down the wrong path

Dave Johnson: relatively new resident of Jesus Creek; he and his wife, Martha, have donated much of their time to improving the quality of life in town

Jason: a mysterious rider

Henry Mooten: the new mayor (Yep, he won the election!)

Mr. Proctor: owner of a gas station; a gentle, well-bred man with the heart of a saint

Jennifer Atwater: local girl who married early and is about to be surprised by the turn her life takes

Billy Atwater: Jennifer's adoring husband, who will be equally surprised

Maedyne Jackson: Jennifer's meddling mother

Mrs. Law, Mrs. Lambdin, Mrs. Healy, et al: don't worry about them, they only appear once

Animals

Minerva: the Tea Room cat

Purrsey: Mrs. Law's neutered tabby

Bella: Kay's mixed-breed, spayed cat

Sundance: the lovely little Palomino ridden by Kay

Shadow: the horse that scared Reb

Pancho: a paint who is wilder than he looks

Pudding / Comanche: one horse, one personality, but ridden by German, who must enjoy confusing man and beast alike

CHAPTER 1

IN JESUS CREEK THE GRAND OPENING OF A new business is cause for celebration. To keep this in perspective, though, you have to realize we would have celebrated the addition of another lawn ornament in Frankie Mae's yard with equal enthusiasm. Ah, simple pleasures.

At least half the town turned out on a hot night in early August to enjoy the open house at Trina's Tea Room. Ordinarily, an outsider like Trina would have been treated with a certain amount of reserve and the crowd might even have been smaller because of her alien status, but Trina came to us via her husband, Bruce Bradley.

The Bradleys are an old family in this area, with their roots reaching back to wrap around the scrawny throats of the original settlers. Bruce had grown up in Jesus Creek, gone off to some faraway university to get his business degree, then married an out-of-state girl and brought her home to meet the clan. Not the choice I'd have made—dragging someone I care for into this quaint but stifling garden spot—but perhaps Bruce had tremendous

1

faith in Trina's ability to tolerate the unusual, even
bizarre, behavior of his friends and neighbors.

They'd moved into a small rental property three
months before and gone immediately to work on the
Tea Room. Every time I rode by there, I'd see them
sanding or painting or hauling in furniture. They'd
started publicizing the Tea Room a month before,
gearing up for this one grand evening. They'd done
it all just right, but word around town was that the
Tea Room was destined to fail.

The official start time for the party was seven
P.M., but most of us here in Jesus Creek have failed
to grasp the concept of fashionably late, and by the
time I rode up to the Tea Room at six forty-five, the
doors were already open and folks were milling
around inside. I tied Sundance to the hitching post
out front (like most of the businesses in town,
Trina's offered this courtesy for the newly mounted
police force) and joined the group.

I knew them all, of course, because I've lived in
Jesus Creek all my life and the town just isn't that
big. Mayor Mooten, decked out in his good suit, was
holding court in one corner. Frankie Mae Weathers
was surreptitiously inspecting the platter of whole
grain cookies. Almost everyone in town seemed to
be either coming through the door or milling about,
and I could see the look of pride on Bruce's face as
he surveyed the room full of happy guests.

"Kay!" Bruce spotted me right away and zig-
zagged through the crowd to welcome me. "I see
you're in uniform. Not here to arrest anyone, I
hope."

When we were classmates at Jesus Creek High,

his usual greeting was a neck pinch that would have done any Vulcan proud, but to this day I flinch when I see him coming. Truth be told, I had a slight crush on him back in our younger days, and it still gave me a little tingle when he came into sight.

All grown up now, Bruce hugged me, and I noticed the smell of a weedy but not unpleasant cologne. I knew from the advertising that Trina's Tea Room would offer herbal preparations, and if that was an example, I'd be doing my Christmas shopping here.

"Nice store, Bruce," I told him. I glanced around at what surely was the classiest looking place in town these days. The Tea Room was in what had once been a clothing store, and the old hardwood floors still creaked and exhaled the comforting musty scent of four decades' worth of dust and foot traffic. There was the underlying aroma of mildew, still lingering from the time a few years back when the Wash-O-Rama next door had flooded half the block, but Bruce and Trina had managed to seal the walls of the Tea Room and paint over the worst of the stains.

The wallpaper they'd put up gave the impression of desert sand in both color and texture, and small area rugs suggested that a Bedouin might charge through the doors any time and settle cross-legged on the floor. I wondered if the rugs were expensive and hoped not, as I'd stepped in a pile of horse poop earlier and still had some of it clinging to my shoe.

The place was brightened and spruced with filmy veils draped from the ceiling, and a magnificent quilt covered most of an end wall. In addition, there were posters advertising herbal remedies, consciousness-altering seminars, private consultations with Trina, and a variety of fortune-telling tools. From the options, I deduced that she was a master of tarot cards, tea leaves, and a number of other divining methods I'd never even heard of.

The oversized, hand-lettered menus tacked up at random offered a selection of nutritious delights such as tofu salad and hearts of artichoke served with tomatoes and hummus on acorn bread. Well, Eloise's Diner wasn't likely to lose any regular customers to the Tea Room. Heck, I wasn't even sure hummus was a food. Of course, the only beverages offered were all-natural herb teas and fruit juices, with fresh springwater (BOTTLED LOCALLY) thrown in for the weak of heart—or stomach.

"Getting this place fixed up was the worst of it," Bruce said, with a proud glance around at his handiwork. "Dad did most of the work. He's the Charlie Daniels of fix-ups. He also gave us a hefty discount on the supplies."

Marty Bradley, Bruce's father, owns a thriving lumber store and is the very embodiment of the term gentle spirit. Bruce could believe that family ties helped him acquire that discount, but the truth was, Marty knocks a few cents off the price for everybody.

And Bruce's mom, Meredith, owns the only florist shop in Jesus Creek. For a woman who never had the advantage of college instruction, she's done well for herself. By keeping her overhead low (she has the shop in the Bradley's garage), she's been able to turn a tidy profit since the day Meredith's Back

Door Florist opened. She isn't a showy woman, so we aren't sure just how wealthy the flower shop has made her, but there's no question that her financial condition is healthy.

Thinking of Meredith reminded me that I'd seen none of the usual congratulations and good luck floral arrangements in the Tea Room. Each table held a centerpiece, but these were small clumps of wildflowers, flanked by a generous assortment of votive candles.

"You've gotten the town's attention," I remarked in reference to the packed house. "To be honest, I wasn't sure how a New Age business would go over in this town."

"Yeah, I wasn't totally confident, either. Especially after Mom's dire warnings about bankruptcy and so forth. She and Trina have had a few, uh, heated discussions about the Tea Room."

Ah. The mother-in-law problem. It didn't surprise me that levelheaded, bottom-line Meredith would disapprove of what might well turn out to be a passing trend. After all, Jesus Creek is a tiny puddle, and how many of its residents are likely to shell out for meditation classes and tea leaf readings? Bruce would probably regret not listening to his mother's wise counsel, but in the meantime he was positively glowing with excitement about his new venture.

"I'm surprised you haven't gotten any flack for promoting black magic. Isn't that how most people see this kind of business?"

In the past few years Jesus Creek had been through a half-dozen bursts of satanic furor. Every dead animal or ill-fortune had been blamed on the mysterious cult alleged to operate among us. For the most part, these rumors were stirred up by one or two hysterical residents, and real crimes kept our small police department busy enough that we hadn't gone looking for evildoers who might not even exist. Still, there remained a few who devoted themselves to the battle against ungodliness, and the Tea Room might have been a prime target for them.

What I knew of this was so little and so vague I saw no point in mentioning it, but personal experience assured me that the rumors were not entirely untrue.

Bruce grinned. "Check the front window. We made a point of displaying a dozen books on Christian spirituality. Trina always says she doesn't care what people believe or worship, so long as it leads toward the greater good. Oh, well, we did get that one phone call this morning. Some crank asking for a quart of bat's blood. Trina gave him a lecture on animal rights."

"Introduce her to Delia Cannon," I suggested, and as the words left my mouth Delia and her significant other, Roger Shelton, stepped through the door.

"Oh, officer!" Roger shouted to me, loud enough to draw the attention of the assembly. "I'd like to report an illegally parked nag."

Roger's tall lanky body always looked disjointed next to tiny Delia, but otherwise they seemed a perfect pair. He amused himself by annoying folks right and left, and Delia humored him while he did it.

Roger and Delia joined us in the corner, with Delia smiling tolerantly at her beloved. She's used to Roger's sense of fun, and I get a kick out of him myself, but we both understand that not everyone finds the man amusing. "Delia, Bruce says that Trina is an animal lover," I said.

"Lover?" Bruce repeated. "We had four dogs when we left home this morning. No telling how many are living with us by now. I swear, every stray in three counties heads right for our door. See?" He pointed toward the other side of the room, where Trina was mingling with a group of dowdy old ladies and holding a gigantic black and white fluffball in her arms. "That's Minerva. Trina's decided she'll be the Tea Room cat, since we already have three at home."

I wondered what my own cat was clawing to shreds at the moment. Bella has never allowed me to cuddle her and she regards with disdain my attempts to coerce her into playful action. She is a great disappointment to me, and I often threaten to turn her out on the street, but so far my concern for unsuspecting neighbors has kept her from becoming a homeless feline. "She's a beauty," I said.

Bruce nodded and gazed adoringly at his bride. "Yeah, she is. I almost fell out of my chair the first time I saw her."

Well, who am I to tell the man I was talking about a cat when he's busy worshiping the woman he loves? Marital bliss is not something I want to discourage.

"Vegetarian?" Delia asked hopefully.

"Gads, yes! Rabid about it."

"Excuse me," Delia said as she drifted away from us and toward her kindred spirit.

"You and I will have to form a club, Bruce," Roger said sympathetically. "A support group. Women who love brown rice and the men who go hungry."

The little window air conditioner was losing a battle against August heat, but still the masses poured through the door. Marty Bradley had to squeeze through the packed bodies to get to us, balancing a silver tray above his head. "Finally got here, son," he said. "Where do you want this?" He held out the platter to show us that it was covered in tiny sandwiches.

"On the big table in the middle," Bruce said, and pointed in the general direction. "Is Mom with you?"

Marty's face instantly turned cautious. "I'm sorry, Bruce. She said she's got a backlog of work to catch up on. Maybe she'll be here later on."

A look of mutual frustration and disappointment passed between them. I suspected that there was more to it than Meredith's work load, but it had been hours since I'd eaten, and those sandwiches looked promising. I decided to keep my nose out of the Bradleys' business and try to find myself a quick dinner.

Roger, for all his complaints about vegetarian recipes, kept step with me as we followed the sandwiches to a table loaded down with edible goodies, trying his best to spoil my good time. "I'd like to report a crime," he said. "Someone stuck an unstamped piece of mail in my box. Brothers of Strength or something like that. No return address, but I think it's a new rock band pushing their latest album."

I didn't tell him that no one even makes albums anymore. "That's a federal offense, Roger," I pointed out. "Not my problem."

Generally around here we can all expect a platter of ham to serve as the centerpiece of any buffet table, but not, obviously, in Trina's. I spotted fresh veggie crudités and a pale brown dip beside them, along with a pile of carob brownies. Trina and Bruce had thoughtfully provided identifying cards beside each treat, otherwise none of us would have known what we were eating. I took one of everything and sampled as I wandered around the room.

Brochures atop a small round table offered information about some of the services to be provided by the Tea Room. Flipping through them, I learned that I could sign up for classes in Beginner Yoga, Astral Projection, and Creative Cuisine. None of those sounded like what I'd been looking for. Where's the brochure on Instant Riches? I wondered.

Every now and then I'd glance out the window to check on Sundance, who is the sweetest horse on earth and who always waits patiently while I go about my business. About half the people who passed him on the way in stopped to pat him, and the few who were leaving offered him carrots filched from Trina's refreshment tray. He's spoiled rotten and sometimes I wonder if a cop's horse ought to be the town pet, but what can I do? It seems the only person who doesn't adore Sun is my own true love, Wayne. He, like our grumpy old police chief, believes that horses exist only so glue can be manufactured.

I'd lost track of Bruce, but at least he knew I'd been there. I was thinking of heading out to continue my patrol when Trina's mingling brought her over to me, presenting my first opportunity to introduce myself.

"I've been dying to meet you!" she sang out in cheery response to my wave. Trina's long black hair shimmered and her lavender, ankle-length skirt danced around her tiny frame. "Bruce says you're the first woman police officer they've ever had here. Is it difficult? Do the men give you trouble?"

"Constantly. But not the way you mean. Reb Gassler, our chief, acts like my father sometimes. And German, who works day shift, is operating on half power, so having a conversation with him is the most stressful part of my job. Then we've got this new guy, Bernie, who's barely out of diapers, and he's so incompetent he thinks the rest of us are gods."

Trina's laugh sounded like a gentle breeze through silver chimes. "You'll have to pick up a sample of my stress-reducing tea. Catch me before you leave and I'll give you a double batch. But don't tell Bruce. He'll lecture me about profit."

So Trina wasn't as business-oriented as her husband and his family. I could imagine the joy Meredith must have felt when she learned of this union. Being one of those people who doesn't understand the concept of a balanced checkbook, I decided that Trina was my kind of people.

Marty came toward us with a celery stick in his

hand. "I'm going to give Meredith a call," he said to Trina. "Maybe I can persuade her to come down here after all."

Trina bit her upper lip and nodded. "Yes, do try."

Marty put a hand on his daughter-in-law's shoulder, as if making a solemn promise, and headed toward the back room to call home.

"It's a shame Vanessa can't be here," Trina said with a sigh. "Bruce is having fun, but he'd really looked forward to having his entire family here to share it with him. But when Vannie has one of her dreadful migraines, she simply isn't able to function."

"Vanessa has migraines?" I asked. It's a wonder Trina understood me, since I'd just discovered that I really liked zucchini sandwiches and had stuffed half of one in my mouth.

"Yes, and they're horrid. She has a strong pain-killer to take, but combined with her regular medication, it knocks her out completely. There's not a chance she'll be able to join us. Poor Bruce." Trina cast a sad glance across the room at her husband, who seemed to be enjoying the event with or without the presence of his female relatives.

From all this you might have concluded that the Bradleys are not a close family. You couldn't be more wrong. Take Vanessa, for example. A few months ago she arrived in town, knocked on the Bradleys' door, and announced that she was Meredith's long lost daughter. As far as any of the rest of us know, there wasn't an ounce of shock or denial. Meredith and Marty took her in, called Bruce home from college to meet his sister, moved her into the extra bedroom, and immediately told the whole town what had happened.

"I was so young and foolish," Meredith had said to me, "and obviously getting pregnant was a serious mistake. I decided right then that I wasn't going to compound it by trying to raise a child when I was still a child myself. Ask Vanessa. I made sure she was adopted by a wonderful couple, and her life with them has been good."

Having met Vanessa a few times, I had to admit that Meredith had made the right decision. The newest addition to the Bradley family was charming, well-educated, a bit outspoken but not rude, and seemed to fit right into the unit.

No one had said why she'd suddenly decided to track down her birth mother or what her adoptive parents thought of the idea, but I guessed she simply wanted to know where she'd come from. Frankly, though, I worried about the people who'd raised her. If I'd supported a kid, changed dirty diapers, put up with teenage tantrums and the expenses of school, clothes, and so forth, I'd have been furious to find that child going in search of a woman who'd merely given birth. Is that unreasonable?

Just then my beeper chirped and I headed for the door. In theory I'm supposed to call the dispatcher to find out what's happening, but Marty was already on the phone and the police department was only a half block away. After dark I'm leery of riding—I'm still kind of new at this equestrian cop business—but it was only seven-fifteen and still full light outside. I hopped on my little palomino and took advantage of the official (until I learned

otherwise) police emergency to canter the wrong
way down Primrose Avenue.

It turned out to be another Jason sighting. For
more than a year now the mysterious Jason has
been a thorn in my side. We suspect he's from out of
town, as no one has responded to our pleas for information about him. Around here there's always
someone who knows everybody's business, but
Eloise swears she hasn't a clue. If Eloise doesn't
know the story, it hasn't happened yet. Then again,
I've seen her leaving full meals in Styrofoam boxes
on the back steps of her diner, and you can't tell me
she doesn't know where it goes.

He rides a motorcycle, this much we know. He
breaks into houses when the owners aren't home
and steals the most ridiculous items—peanut butter,
magazines, like that. When he first became a
problem, his take was more ominous and included
weapons and pawnables, such as VCRs and portable
phones. It's a long story and I won't waste time on it,
but these days Jason takes little things, then disap-
pears into thin air as far as anyone can tell. We
aren't even sure his name is Jason—we call him that
because Reb Gassler scared him right out of his
bike helmet one time and that was the name painted
on it.

I've come this close to catching him a few times,
but always lost him when he takes his bike into the
woods or through an area that wouldn't be safe for
Sundance. As much as I want Jason, I refuse to risk
my little horse for it.

"The Veatches had already left home," Bill the

dispatcher told me, "and Mrs. Veatch remembered that she'd left the coffeepot turned on. So they went back and spotted him breaking open the back door. Jason took off across their yard, crossed Primrose and kept right on going into the woods behind there."

I wondered if Trina's stress tea would have kept my blood pressure down right then. It was clear to me that Jason had been within a few yards of me while I partied at the Tea Room, and that I'd missed him. Of course, I should have been used to the feeling—he'd escaped by a hair so many times I was beginning to wonder if we were letting him get away.

I should have known he'd strike during the party. Jason times his raids for the periods when the town is wide open. A funeral, a wedding—any time the majority of residents are away from their homes, we are vulnerable.

"How many times does this make for the Veatches?" I asked.

"Four," Bill said. "I don't know why they don't just leave the door unlocked like everybody else does. That way they wouldn't have to keep getting it repaired."

Bill had a point. Most of the rest of us (and Jason's helped himself to my pantry, too) have stopped trying to protect ourselves from the boy. He has no objection to breaking in doors or windows to gain entrance. At first some folks tried buying dogs to scare him away, but he must be one of those people with whom animals have an affinity, because we've never found blood or scraps of his clothing at

the scene of the crime. Judging from the content-
ment of some of those animals when I arrive in
response to the call, I'd guess Jason's carrying high-
quality pet food to deactivate just such a security
system.

"Okay," I said without enthusiasm. "I'll ride out
that way and see if I can spot anything. Beep me if
there's a real crime."

I stormed out of the PD angry at Jason, at myself,
and at half the rest of the civilized world. "Stupid,
stupid," I fumed, but Sundance ignored me. "If he's
gonna cause us this much trouble, he could at least
steal something with resale value. With Eloise
feeding him, and twenty other people leaving
clothes and household items on their front porches
for him, why does he have to steal anyway?"

Perhaps the offerings weren't all that he needed.
If Jason could be persuaded to leave us a wish list,
we could all pitch in and provide him with an
easy, comfortable existence. I believed his takings
had less to do with his needs than with the act of
stealing. Jason liked outwitting us, I was sure of
that. Little did he know that I'd taken his criminal
acts as a personal challenge, and that I was determined to stop him or die trying.

Wayne says I waste a lot of time worrying about
Jason, and he's probably right. It's not as if these
are serious breaches of the law, and for that matter,
no one would blame the police department for
ignoring them altogether. Reb has all but told me to
go about my business and leave Jason alone. Still,
I've got this uniform and badge, and I haven't been
on the force long enough to get mellow. That's what

Reb says anyway. So off I went into the woods, in search of a petty thief who's grown into something like a legend in Jesus Creek.

There was a time not so long ago when just sitting on Sundance made my stomach knot up with terror. It sure isn't something they train you for at the academy. Who knew that when Henry Mooten made that campaign promise—"Reliable transportation for the police department"—he was talking about livestock?

I'd taken my riding lessons very seriously, showing up for every one even when the temperature fell way below freezing, and while I wasn't likely to make the Olympic team, I could finally handle myself with a wee bit of confidence.

Reb, on the other hand, refused to have any part of it. Our chief about had a fit when he was presented with this huge Tennessee Walking Horse named Shadow. In fact, he had what is commonly termed a hissy fit and fought every attempt we made to persuade him of the logic behind Mayor Mooten's unique solution. About a week after his first lesson, Reb fell off the horse (although he swears he was thrown, and there *is* a difference) and Shadow took off without him. Reb spent the next hour or so roaming around town on foot, asking people, "Have you seen my horse?" That experience was so traumatic, he's never gotten in the saddle again. He patrols Jesus Creek on foot, leading Shadow behind him because Mayor Mooten insists that a mounted policeman must have a horse and that Reb cannot, must not, and will not, leave his steed back in the pasture.

Mooten made a deal with Rhonda, a local woman who loves horses and keeps taking them in, but who hasn't enough time to ride each and every one herself. For a small rental fee the department gets horse, tack, and feed, and the animals get to travel interesting new paths instead of hanging around Rhonda's farm all the time. With the money we no longer waste putting Band-Aids on the patrol cars, we've been able to hire another full-time officer. You'd think the chief would be grateful to old Shadow, since having an extra officer allows Reb to take time off now and then. Ah, but Reb Gassler is a stubborn man, set in his ways and determined to be a royal pain about this, no matter how sensible it is to have a mounted patrol.

The houses on the west side of Primrose back up to acres and acres of woodland that's owned by a logging company. Kids on four-wheelers have carved out trails that are just perfect for horseback riding—and for Jason's motorcycle, I suppose. I picked a trail at random and slowed Sun to a walk, looking for signs that Jason might have come the same way, all the time itching to trot or canter instead. After about twenty minutes of nothing more interesting than a feisty squirrel, I gave in and nudged Sundance into a trot.

You can't go too far in a straight line around here without running right into the next county, but the trails twist and turn and wander for miles, going nowhere at all. The fun of riding those trails had been tempered, though, after a game warden was shot, apparently mistaken for a deer by some careless hunter. I made a point of wearing a blaze orange cover on my helmet, but who knows if that will be enough to stop a twitchy trigger finger?

I spent at least an hour working Sundance into a lather, but when the last trace of light disappeared behind the hills, I figured I'd better play it safe and walk slowly back to town. By my watch, it was just before nine o'clock when my beeper called me back to reality. I sighed and turned Sundance around to head back to town, thinking that if it was just another Jason sighting, I would probably pitch a hissy fit myself.

When I got to the PD, Bill was pacing back and forth in his little office. "What took you so long?" he demanded.

"I was in the woods," I said shortly. "And I don't have a winged horse. Now what's the problem? You've interrupted what promised to be a lovely evening ride."

"There's big trouble over at the Bradleys'," he said, tossing his head from side to side. "Somebody's been killed!"

CHAPTER

2

THE BRADLEY HOUSE WAS AN UNPRETEN-
tious white frame with two sedate stories and an
attached garage. It had been built in the 1950s and
meant to suggest stability and success. Two exactly
placed maples anchored the trim yard and provided a
comfortable barrier against summer sunlight. After
dark the trees loomed like giant shadow guardians,
unaware that they'd been remiss in their duties.

Marty's car was in the driveway, scooched over to
one side to allow room for customer parking.
Meredith had compromised by allowing Marty to
park in his own drive, but that's where she drew
the line. Bruce's car, I noticed, was parked on the
street.

Marty, Bruce, and Trina were huddled together
on the front porch. When I stopped at the end of the
driveway and tied Sundance to a tree, Bruce left the
group and walked across the immaculate yard to
meet me. "Someone's killed my mother," he said
simply.

I'd been so certain that Bill was mistaken,
thinking perhaps one of Trina's animals had been
hit by a careless driver and she'd overreacted.

Barring that, I might have accepted the possibility that Vanessa had overdosed on her headache pills, but Meredith Bradley dead I wasn't prepared for. "Huh?" I said.

"In the flower shop." He pointed toward the garage directly in front of me. "Dad found her. He wouldn't let Trina or me go in there. I'd have done it anyway, but he's in bad shape and I didn't want to argue with him, or do anything to make it worse."

I looked over at Marty Bradley and saw that he was trembling and being supported by Trina. Marty's a big guy, and my first thought was that Trina must be stronger than she looks because he certainly seemed to be depending entirely on her to keep him upright.

"How about you?" I asked Bruce quietly. "Are you okay?" His color was bad and the porch light cast skeletal shadows on his face.

"For the moment," he said, recognizing that when the shock wore off, he'd need as much help as his father. Like Marty, Bruce is tall and stocky, but just then he looked like a stiff breeze would blow him away.

"Let's go join them, then," I said. I didn't envy Trina the role she'd be playing over the next few days—nursemaid, mommy, and psychologist to both those men. She'd see the worst of her in-laws before she'd even had a chance to settle into the new family.

Trina was trying to convince Marty to sit down but he kept shaking his head and staring alternately at trees and shrubs, now and then gazing off into the night sky. I wasn't in much better shape than any of them, frankly, and it was a chore to think straight and get the basics taken care of.

The Jesus Creek Police Department doesn't often deal with death. Most of our town's residents are neatly tucked away in the hospital when they expire, leaving the details for doctor and family to sort through.

I'd been on the force only a few years and had handled a couple of fatal traffic accidents, but Bruce's assertion that someone had killed his mother was a first for me. If Meredith really had been murdered, I'd have to take on responsibilities that were entirely unfamiliar. I felt a sudden kinship to Trina.

Bruce went to his father and shifted the burden onto himself, while Trina looked at me, silently pleading for help. They expected a lot, and I wasn't sure I had enough to give. "I need to know," I said, and tried to remember what. "I need to know exactly what happened."

Bruce and Trina looked at Marty, who didn't seem inclined to answer me. At last Trina said, "We came back here together, right after the last customer left. It's been such a long day that Bruce and I decided to leave the cleaning up at the Tea Room for tomorrow, so as soon as the last guest left, we locked the doors and rode over here. We were going to tell Meredith all about—" She glanced at Marty to see if the mention of his wife's name might set him off, but Marty showed no sign that he'd heard.

"Trina and I planned to head for home later," Bruce said, picking up the tale. "We were in the kitchen—we'd brought some of the leftovers from the grand opening and we were putting those down on the table. Mom wasn't anywhere in the house, so Dad went to the shop to get her, and then he came back out and told us."

"I see," I said. I didn't want to push Marty too far, either. "So you've all been in the kitchen and Marty's been in the flower shop. Did you go anywhere else?"

"Well, we came in through the front door and through the living room, down the hall to the kitchen. I used the phone there to call for help," Trina said.

"You're absolutely sure about this?" I asked, meaning, Are you sure Meredith is dead and not just napping?

Marty finally looked at me and nodded his head sadly. "Oh, yes," he said.

"And what about Vanessa?" I asked. "Where is she right now?"

That got their attention. All three of them looked at each other and their faces simultaneously broke into expressions of horror. It was clear that they'd forgotten all about this long-lost family member. "She must be in the house!" Marty said to Trina.

All of us knew what he was thinking. Vanessa had gone home from work with a headache and no one had seen her since. She could be dead, or the killer might still have been inside the house. Either way, going in there was not something I had a burning desire to do. Unfortunately, it seemed to be my job.

"Here's what I want you to do," I said to them all. "Stand out here in the yard while I go in and look around. If I'm not back with you in ten minutes, or if you hear anything that doesn't sound right, hightail it over to the neighbor's—" I looked across the street to make sure Delia's lights were burning. "—and tell her to call the PD. Tell Bill to call German. Got that?"

Bruce and Trina nodded. Marty seemed to understand that nothing was expected of him, so he just kept on floating. I hoped I wouldn't be acting the same way once I'd seen the corpse. No one had mentioned cause of death, and I didn't want to discuss it in front of Marty until I'd gotten a better idea of the situation, but my imagination was doing wonders with the possibilities.

I stepped over the threshold and unsnapped my holster at the same time. It occurred to me, in one of those improbable flashes that I hadn't done any target practice in months. The noise bothers me, so I put it off, and Reb doesn't make it a priority, either. The gun felt heavy in my clumsy hand, as if I were wearing mittens, and I realized that sheer, paralyzing terror had numbed my fingers.

I took my time in the living room, looking inside the front closet and behind the furniture. Proceeding down the short hallway to the kitchen, I listened hard for any sound that would alert me to the killer's presence so I could turn tail and run outside. It was, if you'll forgive me, deathly quiet in that house.

The kitchen was spotless in the bald glare of an overhead light. Trina's party snacks sat on the kitchen table, some covered with plastic wrap, some already opened and ready to be enjoyed. The door between the kitchen and the garage/flower shop stood wide open, daring me to take a peek.

I crossed the room on tiptoe and stopped just short of the door, trying to see as much of the shop as possible before entering that room. To my right was the big cooler where Meredith kept cut flowers, the heavy door standing partially open. The door that served as entrance to the shop was to my left and slightly ajar. Just this side of it was a large wooden worktable, where Meredith practiced floral magic. I expected that Meredith would be there, too, probably between the worktable and her desk.

After a few seconds during which not even a tiny whisper came from the shop, I stepped cautiously over the threshold. The whole place was a mess, with flowers, papers, and assorted bows strewn across the floor and the surface of the table. I'd have preferred not to step on any of it but I had to get a look at the body and it just wasn't possible to avoid all that debris. I did my best staying on tiptoe and moving as carefully as I could while keeping my gun at the ready and swinging my head from side to side, the better to watch for homicidal maniacs.

Meredith had never splurged on a real desk. Instead she used a card table, and that's where she kept her cash register. While she hadn't wasted a cent on nonessentials, Meredith had fallen victim to high-tech-itis; in addition to the cash register, the little desk held a computer with laser printer, a fax telephone, a Caller ID unit, and an answering machine on which the light was blinking merrily. I felt sure Meredith would never have updated her operation if all those items had not been tax deductible.

I leaned over the worktable without touching it and saw nothing except more scattered paper and a bulb catalogue that had soaked up a small amount of blood. Meredith had circled a Noel Weston lily, highlighting the price of the bulb in yellow. It wouldn't have surprised me to learn that seeing the cost of that single flower was what had killed her, but who knows—to people with green thumbs, that price might have been perfectly acceptable.

It did strike me that something was missing from the picture—a body. For a brief, optimistic moment I thought that I'd been the victim of a nasty practical joke, but then I turned around and glanced toward the floor. Sure enough, there was Meredith stretched out on her back in the cooler, her legs sticking out from the knees down. With the door half open like that, it was no wonder I hadn't seen the body when I'd first entered. I wished my search had been less thorough.

She had a receipt spindle sticking in her chest. The receipts were still on it. There was a faint trail of blood leading from the body back to the desk, just blobs here and there. The spindle, of course, would have been on the desk, so I deduced that she'd been killed there, probably while sitting down, and that her body had been dragged across the room to the cooler.

I tried to tell myself that it wasn't strictly necessary to examine the body, since I could see perfectly well that Meredith was dead. I knew, though, that there might be a vital clue, so I retraced my steps and knelt down beside the body. Nothing there gave me more information. She was cold, but so was everything else inside the cooler, including me. There was no obvious sign of injury except for the one that had killed her. Nothing to make me think she'd been raped, thank goodness. At least her family wouldn't have to cope with that on top of everything else.

Standing up, I took another look around the shop. Even though I'd been careful to step lightly, I'd still managed to shuffle some of the floor debris, and that bothered me immensely. When the killer dragged Meredith's body across the room, why hadn't the papers and flowers on the floor been disturbed? It occurred to me immediately that the mess must have been made after the murder was committed. Either Meredith had come into the room before a search had begun, or someone had made an attempt to suggest that the killer had been interrupted by Meredith, who'd then been killed as a consequence of her intrusion.

So, I said to myself, she didn't walk in on the robbery. She was here before it began. Had someone come into the shop, ordered flowers, and then decided to rob the place? Or had someone come into the shop especially to kill Meredith Bradley and then tried to make it look like robbery was the initial crime? That possibility sent a chill right down my spine.

I got out of there as quickly as I could and checked the other rooms downstairs—bathroom, dining room. Nothing anywhere appeared to have been disturbed, nor did I find anyone hiding in the breakfront.

Taking the carpeted stairs one at a time, I heard my heart pounding in spite of the roar in my ears. Bruce's old room was at the top of the staircase, and I checked it first, looking in the closet and under the bed. I even pulled out drawers, only to find them completely empty. Meredith clearly was not one of those mothers who keeps her little boy's room just as he left it when he went away to college.

The master bedroom, sparsely furnished in shades of beige and tan, was as neat and clean as the rest of the house, and was thankfully free of killers. A knitted afghan added a touch of color, with its deep blue yarn, but the only unexpected piece in the room was a good Martin guitar propped in one corner. I checked the bathroom, putting off until last the third bedroom, the one that Vanessa would have been using.

Just like I'd been taught, I stood to one side of the bedroom door, turned the knob slowly, and threw it open, at the same time gripping my gun and preparing to dive. Silence. As slowly as my adrenaline-hyped body would let me, I leaned around the door frame and looked inside. This room was not as tidy as the rest of the house, but it still beat my house-keeping by a mile. A pair of jeans and a T-shirt were piled on the floor, and on the bed, dressed only in her underwear, was Vanessa. She was snoring. I've never felt such relief in my entire life.

Realizing that it would do her migraine no good if she woke to find an armed police officer standing over her, I went quietly back downstairs and out the front door. The family looked up expectantly.

"Vanessa is sleeping," I told them. "Maybe one of you could wake her and bring her downstairs."

"I'll do it!" Trina volunteered so eagerly I couldn't help thinking she was desperate to get away from her husband and his father. Who could blame her?

"Trina," I said before she could get through the door, "don't touch anything. Not a thing, you understand?"

She nodded solemnly, a product of the television age grasping the importance of fingerprints at the crime scene.

"Both of you sit down here on the porch," I said to the men. Bruce and Marty looked as if they might drop at any minute, and I didn't want to waste time reviving a fainting victim. I must have sounded fairly intimidating, because they obeyed without complaint.

"I'm sorry I have to put you through this, Marty," I said, "but I need to know. When's the last time you saw Meredith today?"

Marty smiled his forgiveness at my brutality. "About fifteen of seven. Before I left for the Tea Room."

I thought back to the grand opening. "You couldn't have gotten to the Tea Room before five or ten after seven," I told him. "I remember when you came in. You brought food. But it's only a two minute walk from here at most."

"Yes, but I didn't go straight there," he said. "I drove over to Bruce and Trina's to pick up those snacks."

"I called him about six-thirty," Bruce said, "and asked him to do that. We had so much going on today that Trina and I both forgot about the tray of potato sandwiches, and we especially wanted to serve those."

"So at six-forty-five or six-fifty, Meredith was fine?"

Marty sighed. "Yes. She was in the shop, working as always. She's tireless." He smiled a little at the memory.

"Was there a customer with her? Or was she expecting a customer?"

"Not that late in the day," Marty said definitely. "The shop always closes at five, but Mere keeps on working until she's caught up for the day. She never leaves anything over, and often she'll make up arrangements ahead. Silk flowers keep forever."

"Maybe one of the neighbors saw somebody go in," I muttered to myself.

"All the neighbors were at the Tea Room," Bruce pointed out. To back up this claim, a shiny new Ford pulled into the driveway next door. The neighbors were home and they hadn't missed the commotion in the Bradley yard—they stared without apology, but none of us waved them over.

I hadn't wanted to ask earlier, but now I had a murder on my hands and I couldn't afford to be polite any longer. "Bruce, why wasn't your mother at the opening? Surely she'd have left a little work undone in order to be there for you."

Marty gave his son a sympathetic look, then said to me, "Mere didn't approve of Bruce's business venture."

"Why not?" I asked, surprised. "I'd have thought she'd be tickled to see him go into business for himself. She's always been so proud of his grades and of his business degree."

"Oh, yes. Mere's extremely proud of Bruce. As am I. But this wasn't the sort of business she approved of."

Bruce recognized the confusion on my face and explained. "It's the idea she couldn't stand. She thought the Tea Room was doomed to failure because it's such an . . . ethereal concept, I think she said. And she said it was unethical to sell spirituality. She and Trina never saw eye-to-eye on this and I don't expect they ever would have. Mom was convinced that we would go broke and go to Hell because of the Tea Room."

"So she refused to come to your opening for that reason? Because she disapproved of the type of business you started?"

"That's about it. She even offered to help finance another type of store—any other type—but this is what Trina enjoys."

"What about you, Bruce?" I asked. "I don't remember you ever being interested in herbs and crystals."

"I wasn't until I met Trina. In fact, at first I thought she was way over the edge, but after I got to know her, I could see that the loony bits actually make sense in the right context. Trina's not spacey, and she doesn't let the stars or the spirits run her life. She's just interested in alternative medicine and holistic approaches to health."

"Uh-huh," I said, thinking that Bruce was well

and truly smitten. "So at six-forty-five, Meredith was fine? Right, Marty?"

Marty nodded.

"And Vanessa was here when you left home?"

The question seemed to puzzle him. "No, she wasn't," he said.

"Vanessa called us at the Tea Room around six-thirty, just after I'd talked to Dad about picking up the snacks," Bruce put in. "She was at the lumber store then and she said she had this dreadful headache and was going home as soon as she finished shelving the last of whatever came in today."

Vanessa had been working in Marty's lumber store since shortly after she'd come to town, and by all accounts she was doing a good job there. Customers, particularly older male customers, were amused when they found themselves being waited on by a female. Imagine a woman knowing all about shelving board! Wayne had even mentioned it once. He'd said she knew more about lumber grades than he did, and that if it hadn't been for Vanessa, he'd have bought the two grade instead of the one grade or some such thing.

"Can we assume, then, that Vanessa came home no later than seven o'clock?" I asked.

"That sounds about right," Bruce agreed.

"And then I called Mere a little after that," Marty said, "to ask her again to come to the opening. But she didn't mention Vannie being here then."

"That's right. You called from the Tea Room just before I got the Jason beep. About seven-fifteen."

Marty shrugged, as if it didn't matter, and it probably didn't. Almost two hours were left unac-

counted for between the time he'd called Meredith
and the time he'd found her body. I was very much
afraid we wouldn't find anyone who could narrow
down the possible time of death any more than that.

"I tried to talk her into coming to the Tea Room,"
Marty said to his son. "If only she had done that . . ."

Yes, I thought. If only you'd done that, Meredith.
If only you'd given in and attended your son's grand
opening, you'd probably still be alive and your
family wouldn't be hanging a wreath on their business doors tomorrow.

Which reminded me: when the only florist in town
is the cause of the funeral, who makes the wreaths?

The next door neighbors were unashamedly
watching us through their windows. Turning back
to Bruce, I said, "I'll have to use your phone." I
didn't explain that I would have to call in the
coroner and get the procedure started. "I want all of
you to go to Delia's for a few hours."

"Sure," Bruce said.

He stood and helped Marty to his feet. When a
shadow fell across us, we all looked up with startled
gasps. We'd forgotten about Trina and Vanessa, but
there they stood in the doorway. Vanessa was
groggy, but at least dressed in the jeans and shirt
I'd seen on her bedroom floor.

Trina was guiding her toward us, and Vanessa,
with her wrinkled clothes, mussed hair, and her
drug-glazed eyes, looked half mad. I watched her
trying to rub life into her sleepy face and realized
that, as far as any of us knew, Vanessa had been the
only other person in the house when the murder
was committed.

* * *

Even Roger, generally full of irreverent good cheer, can be counted on to say and do the right thing when circumstances turn solemn, so I left the Bradleys in his and Delia's capable hands. I used Delia's phone to call Bill and direct him to alert all the proper authorities, then I returned to the Bradleys' alone.

Sundance snorted and pawed the ground when I reached into my cantle bag to retrieve my camera. "Sorry, little buddy." I whispered, lest anyone notice me talking to a dumb animal. "But you'll have to wait a while." Feeling guilty about neglecting him, I untied his lead rope and moved him to another tree where he could nibble on a fresh patch of grass.

The Jesus Creek police force is a skeleton crew at best. One officer per shift can just about handle your basic daily schedule—a fender-bender here, a domestic squabble there. For the most part, though, the townsfolk watch out for themselves and each other. And lucky they do, I thought as I entered the Bradley house again. It was clear that the entire evening shift of the JCPD would be busy for the next little bit.

Having placed my phone calls to the appropriate authorities, I steeled myself and prepared to do my duty as a law enforcement official. The front door opened directly into the living room, with no charming foyer to welcome guests. Just like Meredith. Skip the opening frills and get right to the point. This wasn't one of those plastic-covered, company-only living rooms, either. The television at the far end of the room was the focal point, with a well-worn recliner, the study, tweed-covered sofa and matching chair arranged around it.

I could tell that Meredith had claimed as her spot the tweed chair—her needlework basket was on the floor beside it. She'd been knitting a sweater from muddy-brown yarn, and I didn't suppose anyone would be finishing the project for her. Marty, then, must use the recliner, because the end table next to it held a collection of music, fishing, and travel magazines. There was nothing to suggest that Vanessa had ever been in this room, much less taken up residence there.

In an ideal world, the entire house would have been roped off, tagged, labeled, photographed, and dusted for prints immediately. In spite of Mayor Mooten's best efforts at community improvement, Jesus Creek is not ideal. Time and resources (and my own intuition) determined the crime scene to be Meredith's one-room flower shop. If I missed important evidence, the TBI would no doubt find it during their more thorough search, and forever afterward I would be kicking my own butt.

All those goodies from the Tea Room opening still sat on the kitchen table and counter, and as I passed through the room, I heard them crying out to me. "Food poisoning!" they shouted. "Help us!"

Putting my camera down, I gathered up the trays and plates and bowls, and tucked them into Meredith's refrigerator. They'd be safe there, nestled among the clearly labeled, efficiently stacked condiments and leftovers. Meredith must have been going for a Kelvinator Cleanliness award. Even the jars and bottles in the door of the fridge were arranged by size. My own fridge is a jumble of oddities and mold in different developmental stages, so I was a tad intimidated.

The door leading from the kitchen to the flower shop was still ajar, just as I'd found it earlier. I popped a fresh roll of film into the camera and snapped a shot of the door. It's been my experience that the most vital snapshot is the one that doesn't turn out, so I snapped another in deference to Murphy.

Just inside the shop I snapped doubles from every angle, then proceeded carefully across the messy room and recorded the other surfaces—tidy desktop with every item precisely placed, the work counter, a close-up of the bloodstained magazine opened to that lovely-but-pricey Weston lily, a creative shot of the interior of Meredith's trash can. I made three shots of the back door entrance, which was unlocked but snugly closed. The killer hadn't had to break anything to enter, but that told me nothing about the criminal's mind. Meredith had been working in the flower shop when Marty left her, and she'd have kept the place open for business as long as she was there. Never one to turn down a customer (or a profit), Meredith Bradley had been known to open business before dawn in order to accommodate a remorseful husband seeking to restore domestic harmony with the help of a dozen roses.

Normally I am not so conscientious when recording the crime scene, but this was a special case. I wanted the prosecutor to have the best possible chance at conviction. I also wanted to avoid getting near the corpse. Eventually, though, I had only six exposures left in the camera.

Meredith's upper body was inside the cooler, her arms above her head. I suspected that her killer had grasped her wrists to drag her across the room and had then simply dropped her. Her eyes were closed (thank you, Lord!) and a single green frond was stuck to her cheek.

Blood had seeped out of the puncture and dried in a ragged circle on her green dress. The dim light in the cooler made it look as if a huge bud had burst into bloom on Meredith's chest. The spindle, then, would be a deadly thorn in the simile.

I had to step carefully over the body to snap the scene from above her head, and it wasn't the chilly air in the cooler that sent shivers through me. Believe me, I didn't spend a lot of time worrying about framing—I just pushed the button and got out of there as fast as my jelly legs would let me.

By that time I was trembling all over and the prosecutor's case had lost priority. I simply wanted to be finished and back in the saddle, riding hell-bent for leather through the woods.

I used the last three exposures on Meredith's lower body, fighting down an urge to move her sprawled legs into a more ladylike position. One of her sensible shoes had fallen off a few feet from the body, but otherwise there was nothing remarkable about Meredith's lower half. After the film was used, I clicked a few random shots of the room until I heard the camera whir itself out. Reb taught me to do that. "Just keep snappin' away," he'd said. "You can get two or three good pictures off the end of the roll." He'd also taught me to take my own shots, because the TBI sure as hell wouldn't share theirs with us.

By the time I'd finished, the doc had arrived, wearing his I'm-a-regular-guy jeans and T-shirt. Dr. James is full of corny jokes, and nothing gives him more pleasure than directing his stale humor at me. "Looks dead to me," he quipped when he saw me. "Cold, pale skin. Glassy stare."

"Ha ha. Normal people always look like this when we find a corpse. You, on the other hand, are a heartless ghoul."

He flashed me a toothy grin and knelt down beside Meredith's body. "Interesting choice of weapon," he said, clearly intrigued. "Stake through the heart. Perhaps this woman is undead."

"Don't touch anything," I reminded him. "And don't discuss the details with me."

"You need to yank this thing out?" he asked, pointing to the spindle.

"Hell, no! And don't you touch it, either. The TBI can dust it and bag it and sit on it, for all I care."

Not so long ago, we rural police officers were blessed (or cursed) with a dandy new concept in investigation—the Tennessee Bureau of Investigation's Mobile Crime Scene Unit. Because of the TBI MCSU, I could afford to ignore that spike in Meredith's body. The TBI's experts would be along any minute to repeat the steps I'd already taken. Then they'd remove the murder weapon for labeling, gather up every other item that could possibly turn out to be evidence, strip Meredith of her clothing and jewelry, and have the body delivered to the medical examiner for autopsy. In short, the TBI would be taking over the investigation, which pleased me no end.

Oh, sure. We know they sneer at us. They think we're incompetent Bubba cops, and they'll let us know we missed fingerprints or corrupted the scene by breathing on it, but that's okay. We don't mind. Really. You just oughta hear what we say about them.

"Okay. I'm done." Doc came out of the cooler, apparently unaffected by the environment.

"How nice for you," I snapped.

It was unreasonable to be angry at him. Did I really want a coroner who fell to pieces at the sight of a dead body? Absolutely not. Doc came in, did his job, and remained rational in spite of it, just as he should have. I was annoyed because my old friend Bruce had lost his mother, and because Marty would have to learn to live without a wife. I worried about Trina, who would be responsible for the burden of family grief through coming weeks, and I ached for Vanessa, robbed of a parent she'd only just met.

But I was absolutely furious at myself for being annoyed with Meredith about her lime-green dress. I wanted to write a poem about her death—and "rose-red life bled out upon the green" did not sound as good as, say, white would have.

It's how I cope.

Death is such a rotten setup, isn't it? I mean, it's like being in a poker game, but you aren't dealt any cards. What are your chances of winning? Exactly. It's the same with death—eat right, exercise, live clean. You still can't win the game. Well, since being mad about it doesn't do anything except send my blood pressure through the roof, I redirect my feelings in a lot of other (mostly inappropriate) directions.

"I'm going out on the front porch," I told Doc, "to write up my notes and wait for the mobile unit. You can join me if you keep quiet."

"Nothing against your company," he said, stepping over Meredith's legs and toward the door, "but I'm going home. Tell the boys where they can find me." He whistled "Sweet Dreams" as he left.

The porch light was bright enough that I didn't even have to squint. One thing I'm careful about—getting my thoughts on paper. Reb laughs at what he calls my poetic fancies, but that's how it comes into my head and out through the pen.

While I wrote down the facts, modified by vivid adjectives, I mulled over the information that would not go into my notes.

The cash register drawer gaped open, empty of all save three stray pennies, I wrote. Anyone could assume there was money in the cash register, I mused.

There was no obvious sign of forced entry, I wrote. But Meredith would have let a friend or potential customer in even if she'd already closed for the day, I realized.

The impetuous use of the spindle suggests the killer had not expected to encounter the victim, I wrote. He assumed she'd be at the opening of the Tea Room, I knew.

Such a well-publicized event would have been a prime time for one of Jason's excursions. It occurred to me for the first time that no one had reported a single burglary all evening. Why not? The Veatches had scared Jason away just as the grand opening had started. It seemed to me that he might well have moved on to a safer target, or so he'd think, and tried his luck at the Bradley house. He wouldn't have been put off by an open door, since so many of us have stopped bothering to use our locks. Surprised by Meredith, he'd picked up the spindle and killed her, then tried to hide the body by . . .

What's wrong with this picture? I asked myself. You either hide a body or you don't, my self replied. In the cooler or out. Not half and half. Had the killer been interrupted again, before he could finish dragging Meredith into the cooler? Vanessa had gone home with a headache, probably around seven P.M. Maybe she'd frightened Jason—or whomever, I corrected myself—before he'd finished.

If it had happened that way, then Meredith had been killed, the money taken from the register, and then the body moved. Peculiar, and not the way I'd have done it, but not impossible. Clearly the killer had plenty of time to gather up the money, but not to move the body.

All this was speculation, of course, and I was ignoring the obvious conclusion that would have to be dealt with soon.

Meredith knew everyone in Jesus Creek and almost everyone in the county. There are other florists in the nearby towns, but none of them could hold a candle to Meredith Bradley. In addition to her uncanny business sense, Meredith had an eye for floral arrangement. Give her a handful of frost-bitten weeds and she'd turn it into a bouquet so lovely and original it would steal your breath. People traveled dozens of miles to buy their center-pieces from the Back Door Florist. They had to— Meredith never delivered, except for funerals.

If anyone had a complaint about Meredith, either professionally or personally, someone would have known and word would have spread all over town. A robber could easily have copped a better haul from almost any house in town than from the flower shop. There seemed to be no motive at all for Meredith's murder.

I wasn't sure motive was important, though. Generally when you find a dead body in a house and only one other person is known to have been in the house at the time of the murder, an arrest is easily made. I looked across the street and saw Delia's living room lights twinkling at me.

CHAPTER
3

I LED SUNDANCE ACROSS THE STREET AND
tied him to the sturdy oak that lent summer shade
to Delia Cannon's house. We'd left behind evidence
of our presence at the Bradleys', so with Delia's
permission I borrowed a shovel and tidied up,
depositing the organic fertilizer on top of the com-
post heap in Delia's backyard. Sundance watched
me without a trace of interest or remorse evident in
his big brown eyes.

The Bradley family sat in numb silence at Delia's
kitchen table, mugs of untouched herb tea cooling in
front of them. There were several good reasons for
talking to them right away. For one thing, they
were calm, still drifting in the mellow haze of disbelief. As far as Marty Bradley knew, he might wake
up from this horrible nightmare any second and
smile at the restoration of his comfortable life.

For another, the edges of the wound were still
raw. This was the uncensored period when any one
of them might blurt out information that a few days
of emotional shuffling would bury forever. I needed
to ask questions before the story jelled, before eti-
quette reminded them that one doesn't speak ill of

the dead. There are innocent victims, and it certainly appeared that Meredith had joined those ranks, but if she'd somehow contributed to her own death, I needed to know right away.

Delia offered me a cup of tea and her seat, then she and Roger discreetly disappeared. Marty and his son watched me sit down with about the same level of interest Sundance had shown during the cleanup operation. I wondered if they realized I was there in my official capacity, and that they were all suspects. Picturing me as a potential adversary was probably as difficult for Bruce as imagining any of them in the role of killer was for me.

Vanessa might well have been asleep, with her long dark blonde hair falling forward to half cover her face. Her hands rested limply on the table. I noticed how sturdy they seemed—square, with blunt-tipped fingers and sensibly short nails. Meredith's fingers had been long and tapered, the sign of an artistic personality, or so claimed my high school art teacher.

Everything about Vanessa, though, suggested that she was an alien child, a changeling dumped at the door. She was tall and thin, with brown eyes that didn't even attempt to fight off whatever painkiller she'd taken. Meredith had been shorter, with a rounded body that would never have appeared svelte no matter how she dieted. I couldn't find a single similarity between Vanessa and her biological mother, and it set me to wondering what Vanessa's father looked like. I wondered, too, if Vanessa had contacted him, or if she even knew who he was.

Meredith had been open about her unexpected pregnancy, but she'd said nothing at all to identify the other person involved. I had no doubt that one of the town wags would remember who Meredith had been dating back in those days, so finding out more about Vanessa's biological background wouldn't be too difficult.

Trina, pale and drawn, watched me with all the intensity the others lacked. By default, she was the family spokesperson.

"Anything?" she asked me quietly.

I understood that she referred to my investigation of the flower shop. I shook my head. "People will be coming and going over there for a while," I warned. "When we're finished here, maybe y'all can go to your house."

Trina nodded. "That's a good idea." She placed a gentle hand on Bruce's arm, as if she could infuse strength or draw out pain. "We'll need to get a few things first. Clothes for Marty and Vannie—"

"I'm sorry," I said. "I can't let you go back in the house. You'll have to consider it sealed off for now."

I saw a momentary flash of defiance in Trina's eyes, but it quickly died out when she realized I was in no position to allow favors. The rules dictated procedure, and while gathering clean underwear probably wouldn't hurt anything, I had no choice but to stand firm.

"I know you're all tired, but I have to ask a few questions."

It would be a lot of questions, but I didn't want them to realize how much more they had to get through before they'd be allowed to collapse into soothing sleep or wild, uninhibited grief.

"Let's just go over the times. Now, Marty—" I turned to face the stunned man on my left. "—tell me again what time you left the house."

He pulled himself together with a deep breath, as if preparing to undertake some heavy physical task. "It must have been around six-forty-five. I left the store just after five-thirty. Vannie offered to stay till closing, so I went home to get a shower. Then I asked Mere about going to the opening, but she said she had to work. Right after that I went to Bruce and Trina's to get those sandwiches, and straight on to the Tea Room."

I nodded and wrote it all down in my notebook. Looking up, I said to Vanessa, "Can you tell me what time you got home?"

Her voice was thick and she needed extra effort to form some of the words. "Left the store at six. Had to go to emergency room for Demerol." Her voice could have been swaddled in cotton.

"Vannie's headaches get really bad sometimes," Trina added. "When the regular medicine doesn't help, she goes to the emergency room for Demerol and, as you can see, it really knocks her for a loop."

"Did you talk to your mother when you got home?" I asked Vanessa. I jotted a reminder to check with the medical center about her visit.

Vanessa shook her head slowly. "She had a customer. I took something for my head and went upstairs."

She didn't seem to realize the importance of what she'd just said, but the rest of us latched on to it immediately. If Vanessa had been claustrophobic, she'd have panicked then, as the rest of us leaned in toward her.

"Vanessa," I said, using my easy, girl-cop voice, "who was the customer?"

"I don't know," she said mildly.

"Was it a man or a woman? Can you describe the person?" I was holding my breath.

"I don't know. I went into the kitchen to get a glass of water and I heard Mere in the shop, talking to somebody. I didn't bother her. My head ached so much."

Hopes of an easy resolution to the case seeped out of me, and I slumped back down in my chair. Now we knew someone had been in the shop with Meredith just minutes before Marty called her from the Tea Room. It could have been an innocent customer, or it could have been the killer. Worst of all, it could have been nobody. Vanessa might very well be lying to cover her own crime.

For that matter, how could I be sure she'd taken a painkiller? It's easy enough to fake the effects of drugged sleep. Still, I wasn't prepared to confront her with such a vicious accusation unless and until I had good cause.

"And after that, around seven-fifteen, you called her from the Tea Room," I reminded Marty.

He nodded absently, as if he were concentrating on a physics problem that could instantly bring about world peace and I'd just asked him if he'd care for a cocktail. I touched his shoulder, hoping that would bring him back to us. "Marty, did she mention a customer when you called?"

"No." His voice was raspy, but not yet ragged.

There we had it. Meredith was alive at seven-fifteen, and so far as we know, in good health. I realized that I should have checked those receipts on the spindle in Meredith's chest, but it seemed damned unlikely that her killer would have ordered and paid for flowers that Meredith most certainly wouldn't have had time to arrange before her death.

On the other hand, I thought with a spark of annoyance at myself, the killer might have come in to pick up a previously ordered arrangement, then killed Meredith afterward. I couldn't think of a single logical explanation for doing that, but who expects rational behavior from a murderer?

Well, if the TBI found a full confession, signed and notarized, stuck to Meredith, they were welcome to it. Anybody who gets that close to a corpse deserves the credit.

"Bruce . . . ?" What could I ask that wasn't a waste of breath? I knew where he'd been all evening, and if Bruce had known anything useful, he'd have told me up front.

"I don't know, Kay." He looked at me, pleading for answers. "I can't believe this is happening. Who'd want to hurt Mother?"

Clearly none of us had an answer for that. At least, none that we were willing to express at that moment. It took everything I had to avoid staring at Vanessa. Her foggy behavior in itself was enough to attract curiosity. Being an outsider, and therefore an oddity, made her even more interesting to me, and to others as well, I suspected.

If she'd killed Meredith, I'd have to deduct points

for intelligence, because she surely could have arranged to get herself out of the house before someone arrived to discover the crime. Could the medication have clouded her reasoning ability? I wondered. Or did she think that would excuse her behavior if she did get caught?

There didn't seem to be anything left to ask the family, except for the standard questions that generate standard answers. Meredith had no enemies. No one had threatened her. Her recent behavior had been perfectly normal. I could have written it without even talking to them.

Jesus Creek, after all, is a smallish place. County seat, sure . . . of the smallest of ninety-six counties in Tennessee. Our courthouse is the heart of town, with a dozen uninspired businesses nestled around it like chicks around a mother hen. We had a population explosion a few years back, bringing the total up to about seven hundred full-time residents, all of whom know the others far better than is healthy or desirable.

Frankie Mae Weathers had once marched up to me on the sidewalk in front of the Wash-O-Rama and asked if I was happy with my new toothbrush. I told her I was. Now, in another part of the world, this might have been a remarkable conversation. Here in our little town there was a simple explanation. Frankie Mae had asked the store clerk if the Ortho-Point toothbrush was worth the price. The clerk, remembering that I had purchased that very brand a few days before, suggested that Frankie Mae ask for my opinion.

My point is this: if Meredith had enraged someone,

or if she'd had any indication of impending doom, her friends and neighbors would have known. I would have known.

I tucked the notepad and pencil into my shirt pocket, then stood up and dumped my untouched tea down the sink. To Trina I said, "Y'all stay here awhile. Delia won't mind."

Trina understood the code: strangers are in Marty's house; you don't want to see that. She nodded firmly and picked up her tea.

Delia and Roger were curled up on the sofa in her living room. Roger was playing with her toes, and Delia was pretending to read the latest Susan Rogers Cooper mystery. I knew she was pretending because when I walked in, she closed it and put it down without marking her place. Besides that, I knew she'd already read it and given it a rave review in the library's newsletter.

"They're doing okay so far," I said. "You might want to get rid of them before reality sets in."

"I can handle it," she assured me. "As long as Roger doesn't fall to pieces. He's a fine man, but useless in a crisis."

"You underestimate me, woman," Roger growled. "I'm sturdy and strong and wise."

"They're here," I said. Through the front window I could see the TBI agent's car parked across the street. Even Roger stopped his banter to sigh.

A knock on the door cut into our helpless reverie. Delia opened it and invited Bernie Thompson into the house. Bernie is the rookie cop on the JCPD. I like him for being there, because it means I'm not the rookie anymore. These days Reb and German treat me almost like a grownup, because compared to Bernie, I'm a hardened veteran. I look at the boy now and then and wonder if he'll ever stop being a wide-eyed, hotdogging defender of law and order. I know I couldn't have been that goofy when I first joined the force.

"Bill said you got a dead body!" Bernie boomed.

I shushed him quickly. "The whole family's in the next room," I whispered.

Bernie ducked his head to hide the embarrassed blush that was spreading across his cheeks. He blushes a lot, our Bernie, and beet-red isn't a good color for a fair-haired, blue-eyed former high school fullback. He's the third son of seven children born into a big old Walton-style family. I'll bet they all sit down at the dinner table every day and hold hands to say grace.

I quickly filled him in on what had happened and what I'd done. All the time Bernie was shaking his head in stunned disbelief. "What an awful thing to do," he said over and over. And then he delivered the line I'd been waiting for. "Do you want me to call Chief Gassler and tell him?"

Bernie wants to notify our police chief every time the horse passes gas. When anyone says young people today have no respect for authority, I refer them to Bernie. He always says sir and ma'am, he stands whenever a lady enters the room, and he thinks Reb Gassler is just a notch lower than God on the universal ladder of importance.

"Bernie, Reb is off somewhere in the wilds of Arkansas, happily smelling of fish and other stinky things. We couldn't find him if we tried, and he'd shoot us if we did. Now just relax and let the TBI handle it. Keep your eyes open for Jason, because I seriously want to talk to him, and ask anybody you run into if they know who killed Meredith Bradley."

One thing about Bernie—he can follow instructions to the letter. Anything he learned about a case would be meticulously noted in his sprawling penmanship. Someday he'd make a fine cop, assuming he could avoid trampling the best clues under his eager, size thirteen feet.

The beeper nearly sent me through the ceiling, which suggested that the evening's events had made me a tad more anxious than I'd realized. Delia handed me her new portable phone, and I heard Bernie decline her offer of tea as I punched in the PD number.

Bill filled me in on the problem and asked if Bernie had caught up with me yet. "Some people got no business on a horse," he said and hung up.

He was referring to Bernie's determined but totally uncoordinated attempt at equestrian arts. Frequently Bernie did not get where he was going without a tumble, and it had a lot to do with his choice of steed. He'd insisted on riding Pancho because "he looks like a lawman's horse." I didn't understand what that meant or why it mattered, and Bernie had ignored advice from Rhonda to befriend a slightly more amenable animal, so taken was he with the appearance of his chosen mount. Consequently, Bernie and his horse often parted company, but that did not deter the good-spirited law officer. Frankly, I worried that someday his try-try-again attitude would get him killed.

Glancing at my watch, I saw that it was twenty minutes after eleven and well past the end of my shift. "Well, Bernie," I said with a smile, "looks like your night's starting off with a bang. A spaceship just crashed in the woods out by the Tyler place." I handed him the beeper and watched him go.

Special Agent Mark Warner of the Tennessee Bureau of Investigation was stringing crime scene tape around the perimeter of the Bradleys' yard. I watched him from Delia's front porch, admiring Warner's cool, efficient manner. Murder was his business and he'd had tons of customers, so it made sense that he'd be better at handling it than I. Still, I was envious.

"There you are!" he said when he saw me walking across the street. "I can't believe you just wandered off and left the crime scene unsecured."

"Gosh, Mark," I said. "I'm really sorry, but I had to move my horse. He wasn't happy over there." I pointed to the spot in the Bradleys' yard where Sun had been tethered.

"You had a horse on the grass? You realize, of course, you've compromised my crime scene!" Mark flapped his arms and tore at his hair in mock exasperation.

I cocked my head to one side and tried to adopt a good ole boy attitude. "Look, pal. I've got a Martian mothership down the road just looking for a juicy human snack. And I hear Martians are scared to death of beautiful women, so *I'm* not worried."

"That's right," Mark said, and chuckled. "This is

the place with the loony mayor. You got that landing pad built yet?"

He referred, of course, to another of Mayor Mooten's priorities. Henry had entered the mayoral race only because, as an ordinary citizen, he'd been unable to get anyone to listen to his plans for a UFO landing pad. So far he'd gathered a small band of followers who took turns watching the skies for our alien visitors' arrival, but monetary donations to the landing pad fund were not coming in as quickly as the mayor had hoped.

"I'm officially off duty, but Bernie's out in the woods checking on the UFO sighting. If you promise not to drag this out all night, I'll stay long enough to bring you up to speed."

"Deal." Mark whipped out his official note-taking equipment. "Tell me everything, starting with the part where you vigilantly stood guard at the scene until I arrived and took over."

Mark grew up in a town that could have been cloned from Jesus Creek, so he has a clear understanding of how we must operate, given our limited resources. Certainly I should have secured the house and yard, but then who would have questioned the family? And I couldn't very well have asked them to sit there on the porch for hours until all the business was done, could I?

Even though he's at least ten years older than I am, Mark gives the illusion of high-spirited youth. The two of us had clicked on our first meeting, and since then I looked forward to running in to him. Usually. Certainly I would not have wished to see him in Jesus Creek in his official capacity. In a

little while the rest of Mark's team would arrive,
along with the crime scene van, and they would not
be as reasonable in their approach. They would
expect the JCPD to operate as efficiently as the
NYPD. I was completely in favor of telling Mark all
I knew and getting the heck out of there as quickly
as possible.

"A receipt spindle, huh?" Mark said.

I'd given him a moment by moment account of all
I'd done and had even thrown in a little background,
but the murder weapon was the only point that
really held his attention.

"With receipts still on it," I reminded him. "You
might find something in that."

"Could be," he agreed. "Sounds like spur of the
moment, though. Grab the nearest sharp object. No
planning that I can see went into it."

"So you think someone came into the shop on a
friendly visit, then suddenly and without warning
decided to kill Meredith."

"Um-hmm," he said. "With an argument in between. And you say the daughter was in the house
at the time." He jotted a note about having her
tested for traces of Demerol. "Does she have a history of violent behavior?"

"I don't know," I admitted.

"You don't know?" Mark rolled his eyes at me.

"Well, she's only been here a few months." I went
on to explain the adoption and reunion, feeling a
ball of lead forming in my stomach as I drew the
same conclusions Agent Warner was drawing.

Mark was practically drooling. "Would you agree
that we have a prime suspect?"

I sighed and allowed him a reluctant nod. As much as I wanted to lay the blame on a despicable stranger, logic fairly shouted Vanessa's name. "But what about motive?" I asked.

"Hatred, seething all these years. Revenge on the mother who abandoned her. Or maybe the daughter's a bad seed. How do we know she hasn't offed the adoptive parents? You checked into her background at all?"

"Give me a break! I just got here a couple of hours ago. What do you think, that I run a background check on everybody who comes to town?"

If Vanessa turns out to be the killer, I told myself, I'll damn sure start investigating newcomers.

"Okay, take me through it," he said. "Show me just what you saw and did. Let's try to wrap this up before the dawn's early light."

Mark and I walked through the house together as I showed him exactly where I'd stepped and what I'd seen in my earlier excursion. He was more thorough than I'd been, peeking behind tables and even into the bathroom drains, and all the while jotting down his impressions.

"Where, exactly, were the clothes?" he asked.

We'd reached Vanessa's room, where the bedspread was still rumpled. "Right about there," I said, pointing to the approximate piece of carpet. "Jeans and a shirt."

"Are you sure she was asleep?"

"Well, she was snoring."

"Could've been faking it?"

I was losing self-esteem quickly. All my life I'd been told that good manners are important, that proper behavior will get you anywhere you want to go. No one warned me that one place it can get you is into hot water.

"Maybe. I didn't try to wake her. I was so relieved she wasn't a corpse herself, and given the circumstances, it seemed cruel to have a virtual stranger roust her with the news about her mother."

Mark's training might not have erased his memory of how small towns work, but it still had some effect on his view of people. While I was prepared to believe that everyone was innocent until proven otherwise, Special Agent Mark Warner had his teeth sunk into Vanessa and was clearly annoyed that I hadn't taken a bite myself.

He checked under the bed and found nothing. In Vanessa's closet, along with neatly arranged clothes and shoes, there was a sewing box filled with thread, thimbles, and carefully folded cotton fabric.

"So you left the suspect up here alone while you went back downstairs?"

"Yes," I said. "I asked Trina—Vanessa's sister-in-law—to come up and wake her."

"Allowing the two of them time to dispose of any remaining evidence," he pointed out.

"Oh, now you're calling it a conspiracy! I suppose the whole family could've been in it together. They probably staged that grand opening downtown to provide themselves with alibis. Gee, too bad Vanessa forgot to show up, isn't it?"

"Officer Martin," Mark said, "is it past your bedtime?"

Perhaps I was crankier than usual, but who could blame me after the stressful day I'd had? A murder, a Jason incident, and a UFO sighting constituted at least a month's worth of calls, and they'd all been compressed to fit into one shift. My shift.

"Okay," I grumbled. "I'll agree that Vanessa appears to be the most likely suspect. If you do a thorough investigation, though, I'm sure you'll find others."

"Can you point me toward someone else with opportunity? If the daughter didn't do it, why didn't she hear a noise? Her story seems to be that she slept blissfully away while a murder occurred right below her."

"Sound doesn't travel that well in this house. And besides, if she took Demerol, Vanessa could've slept through an earthquake. She was barely awake when I talked to her."

"Yeah. Right. If you're going to argue all night, let's go back downstairs. Maybe you can argue the corpse out of being dead and we can all go home."

"I'm about to do that anyway," I said, and faked a yawn. I didn't want Mark to know that I was too squeamish to go into the shop again.

"Lucky you. Looks like I'll be here all night. Can I depend on you to take statements from the locals and share what you learn with my team?"

"Naturally," I said. "And you'll check with me before you do anything rash?"

"You may count on my full cooperation," he said, with a half bow.

I left the Bradleys' knowing full well that the TBI would not be consulting with the JCPD unless they needed something from us and had to barter. Before I collected Sundance, I tapped on Delia's door, and when she opened it, I whispered, "Give them the name of a good lawyer."

Wayne was waiting for me when I finally stumbled through my own front door. One week every month his shift swings to match mine and we both go off duty around eleven P.M. We need time to unwind after work, so it fits perfectly—unless, of course, one of us gets stuck working overtime.

"I was just about to go home," Wayne said after he'd kissed me. "Figured Bernie had fallen off his horse again and you were covering for him."

I pulled off my socks and shoes and tossed them in the closet by the front door. There are few pleasures greater than the feel of a cool wood floor on bare feet, but Wayne had managed to provide most of them. My coffee table was covered with the little gifts he often brings me—chips, chocolate, and cola. Wayne himself was the best present of all.

"A little worse than a Bernie Moment," I told him. "Someone killed Meredith Bradley."

I popped open a canned drink, flopped onto the sofa beside him and propped my feet on the table. After the nutritious snacks I'd wolfed down at the Tea Room, my body was crying out for salt and grease.

"The flower woman?" Wayne asked. "You're kidding. Who killed her?"

I adore his confidence in my investigative skills. "I have absolutely no idea. The TBI had just gotten there when my shift ended—that's why I'm late. I had to go over everything I'd done. Anyway, it looks like they're determined to pin it on Meredith's daughter."

"Oh, yeah?" Wayne put an arm around me and pulled me closer to him. "Why do they think it's the daughter?"

He's only been in Jesus Creek a few years, and he has a genetic inability to keep track of gossip. Before I could explain Mark Warner's theory about Vanessa's motive for killing Meredith, I had to remind Wayne of the adoption and recent reunion.

"So," I said in summary, "Mark thinks Vanessa had a huge, festering ball of resentment that finally burst."

"It would've been smarter for her to slip into town and kill Meredith without introducing herself to everybody," Wayne said.

"True. If she'd planned all along to do this, why did she make herself so noticeable? Doesn't make sense, does it?" I mulled that over for a while. "I know Vanessa is the most likely suspect, simply because she was the only one in the house, but I just can't see it. If she wanted to kill Meredith because she hated her—or for any other reason—she could've planned it better."

Wayne offered me a pretzel from his bag while he thought it over. He's the sort of man who contemplates everything, from major life changes to the shirt he wants to wear. All his musing is time well spent, however, because in the end Wayne's perspective is broad enough to cover the full range of possibilities.

It surprises people when they first notice this about him. Wayne doesn't look like a solid,

dependable sort. He has a beard and a ponytail, and
his earring usually dangles. He is not above
spraying the neighbors with a water hose when he's
washing his truck, and he believes firmly in the
existence of Santa Claus.

"Are you sure Vanessa was home when Meredith
was killed?" he asked finally.

"She says she was home by seven and went right
to bed. We know Meredith was killed sometime
between seven-fifteen and nine-thirty, when the
family got home and found her." The pretzels
weren't quite greasy or salty enough to meet my
body's needs, so I grabbed the chips and chocolate
and tore into them.

"How do you know Meredith wasn't already dead
when Vanessa got there?"

"Because Vanessa heard Meredith talking to a
customer," I said. "And because Marty talked to her
on the phone after that."

Wayne scratched at his beard and added my
answers to his data bank. At the same time, I was
occupied with what I considered the question of the
day: why would a seemingly intelligent girl like
Vanessa commit a murder and leave herself wide
open to suspicion? Even if she had a migraine,
wouldn't it have been worth the discomfort to show
up at the Tea Room and give herself something like
an alibi?

"Okay." Wayne sat up straight, signaling that
he'd had a bright idea. "What if the killer imitated
Meredith's voice on the phone?"

"You've seen too many cheap movies," I told him.
"I doubt Marty would've been fooled by someone

imitating his wife's voice. And even if he had, that customer Vanessa heard was right there in the shop. He or she would've seen Meredith's body on the floor."

"Maybe there never was a customer. What if Vanessa killed her mother, then answered Marty's call herself?"

Once Wayne tackles a puzzle, he doesn't back off until it's solved. Sometimes I regretted asking him for ideas, and other times I wondered why he didn't have Mark Warner's job.

"I suppose Vanessa could have imitated Meredith's voice better than anyone else," I conceded. "I've never noticed whether they sound anything alike, but being mother and daughter would make it possible."

Wayne beamed with pleasure at having been able to present me with a clue. "And you know what else?" he said. "Maybe they weren't mother and daughter. Maybe Vanessa made that up to get into the family."

"Why?"

He shrugged as if the answer should have been obvious. "To inherit Meredith's fortune."

"Did Meredith have a fortune? And wouldn't it go to Marty if she did?" I shook my head. "First she'd have to kill Marty and Bruce, so Vanessa herself would be the only remaining heir."

"If she is really Meredith's daughter," Wayne reminded me. "And if she's the only sibling Bruce has."

My quiet evening at home had produced more work for me to do. First thing, I'd have to find out whether Vanessa was really Meredith's offspring, who her father was, and whether or not Meredith had any other illegitimate children. Then I needed to engage Vanessa in conversation so I could try to determine how closely her voice resembled Meredith's.

"Let's not talk about this any more tonight," I pleaded. "I'm already exhausted."

"You want me to go home?" Wayne asked.

"No, I want you to stay. A UFO landed in the woods tonight, and I'm afraid of being abducted by aliens."

"Oh, you've been abducted *lots* of times," he said confidently, "but you have no memory of it."

CHAPTER
4

I KISSED WAYNE GOODBYE JUST AFTER ONE o'clock on Sunday afternoon. Already dressed for work, I headed down to Eloise's Diner to indulge in lunch prepared by someone other than myself. Wayne was more than happy to see me go, too—he had plans of his own for his day off, involving a frozen pizza, a bottle of root beer, and a Three Stooges marathon on Channel Four. Pizza and root beer are, of course, necessities of life, but Wayne disapproves of my sacrilegious opinion of Curly, Larry, and Moe. I put them in the same column with stand-up comics wearing arrows on their heads, but unfortunately, Wayne doesn't share my good taste in entertainment. I like to say we have an open relationship—he's free to watch bad television and I'm free to leave him alone while he does it.

The air outside was heavy with our usual August humidity, but I've found it's easier to handle if I go with it. Rather than fight the force of a Jesus Creek summer, I accept sweat and move on without complaining. I simply refuse to acknowledge my own misery. Could be a Zen concept, I'm not sure.

Blasting cold from Eloise's air conditioner nearly

knocked me over when I entered the diner. Delia
had staked out a table in the corner and was happily chatting with Eloise, who stood behind the
counter with her coffee and trademark cigarette.
They were the only people in the diner, oddly
enough. Normally the postchurch crowd would have
packed the joint.

If you don't count Trina's Tea Room and the
Drink Tank, where pizza is available for takeout or
dining in, Eloise's is the only eatery in town. It was
started by Eloise's father eons ago, and inherited by
the daughter for whom he'd named the place. I
worked there once, as a highly incompetent wait-
ress, and Eloise still depends on me to fill in from
time to time when one of her employees calls in sick.
In exchange for substituting, I get a slight discount
on my meals even when I'm not working there.

"Where's everybody?" I asked, joining Delia at the
table.

Eloise shrugged. "Probably most of 'em are over at
Bruce Bradley's. I hear they can't get into Marty's."

"The TBI may keep Marty's sealed off for a while
yet. And afterward the place will be such a mess no
one will want to go in there."

"Let me know when it's time," Eloise said. "I'll
make sure somebody goes to clean up. No sense in
Marty having to go through that on top of the rest."

I nodded a promise to alert her. From experience
with past tragedies, the women of Jesus Creek had
honed their compassionate skills. A domestic drill
team of determined Samaritans would descend
upon the Bradley house, brandishing brooms and
mops and cleansers. Their flurry of activity would

produce not only a spanking clean house, but a highly efficient schedule of caretakers as well.

For as long as they were needed, kindhearted ladies would oversee the delivery of sympathy dishes, such as green bean casserole and fried chicken, chocolate cake, and potato salad. They would run an assembly line of dishwashers, reheaters, and foil-wrappers. They are always there in time of need, coming and going without fanfare, and they are almost always well past the age of consent.

Maybe there's a secret society that teaches the art of postmortem care of survivors, into which promising caretakers are inducted at a certain age, or after death becomes a fact of life instead of a frightening oddity.

I only know that I haven't a clue how they manage it, and I've never seen anyone my age among their ranks. I've taken to watching them closely in the past few years, and have realized I haven't even a glimmer of the skills needed. I suspect the ladies of the inner circle noticed this, and that I was black-balled long ago.

Menus were on the table but I didn't need to look. Thoughts of funeral food had tuned my taste buds. "Ham, green beans, and potato salad," I said. It didn't bother me to eat pork in front of Delia any-more, not since she'd teamed up with Roger, King of the Carnivores.

Delia, of course, had a salad with lemon juice instead of dressing. She's a petite woman who could easily be mistaken for a teenager from a distance, thanks to a healthy diet and regular exercise. I could have followed her example, but the stretchy riding pants I'd taken to wearing gave me a false sense of my own size—so long as I avoided mirrors.

"How'd the Bradleys do after I left last night?"

"So so," Delia said. "We had a touch-and-go moment when they started to leave and Marty teared up, but Trina handled it. She just took him by the arm and led him to the car without any nonsense. The girl has a feel for what people need—sympathy or discipline."

"You like her?" I asked.

Delia raised an eyebrow in surprise. "Don't you?"

"Oh, sure. From the little I've seen, she's terrific. Bruce is madly in love, Marty obviously likes her a lot. Hard to tell what Vanessa thinks, given that she was drugged to the gills last night, but Trina certainly seems to like her."

"Trina was being protective last night. I think Bruce and Marty were in shock and totally unaware of most everything. Trina was upset, of course, but nothing slipped past her. I don't suppose you found a fingerprint belonging to someone we don't know and wouldn't like if we did?"

I shook my head. "Nothing so far. The TBI may have some luck, if they try. I'd guess they've already decided on the killer and are just putting together their evidence. Did you talk to them about a lawyer?"

"I suggested quietly to Trina that the family call D. D. Maddox. She said she'd call him at home this morning. As soon as he hears about the murder, of course, he'll figure out who the TBI has targeted as their number one suspect. I gather Trina has caught on, too. That's probably why she seemed to be sheltering Vanessa last night."

"Good," I said. "I'm worried about Vanessa. Of course, the prints still might point to a stranger, or someone might confess. Or I could get lucky and connect Jason to this."

"You've really got it in for that kid." Delia sounded as if she disapproved of my attitude.

"Why shouldn't I? It's not so much that he's hit almost every house in town—he stole my soap! There's something too personal about that."

Delia snickered.

"Don't laugh," I warned. "It could be your shower cap next."

"He returned my book," she said. "The paperback he took the first time he hit my house. Brought it back last time and left it on the kitchen table. Maybe he didn't like it, you think?"

"I doubt he can read," I said cynically.

Eloise brought our lunch orders to the table and sat down with us. "Are you running down Jason again? Give the kid a break, why doncha?"

"He's a thief! A common criminal!" I couldn't believe that those two intelligent women had fallen under the spell. "This is no charming Robin Hood we're talking about. In addition to the stolen merchandise—"

"Just little things," Eloise pointed out.

"He's cost some of us a fortune in household repair."

"Pretty much everybody has stopped locking their doors," Eloise reminded me. "That helps a lot."

"I do not consider helping a thief rob you a viable solution to the problem."

Delia and Eloise exchanged a look of amused tolerance, much like the one Reb and I use on Bernie. I knew I wouldn't be able to convince them that Jason was a serious danger to all of us. Like so many people, they thought of him as a puppy whose cute antics offset the occasional mistake on the rug. I saw Jason as a wild mongrel who needed only the right set of circumstances to turn him into a rabid threat to humanity.

"Well, anyway," Eloise said. She could sense my hostility, no doubt, and wanted to divert the conversation away from Jason. "I heard the grand opening at the Tea Room was a big hit. Too bad it ended like it did."

Eloise had never expressed a hint of resentment toward the business that would become her competition. She was wise enough to know that the two were sufficiently different to hold their own clientele without friction. Or perhaps she didn't take the upstart Tea Room all that seriously. Other food-related businesses had come and gone with little notice, but through the years Eloise's Diner had remained a steady source of comfort for us all.

Delia pushed her plate away, half the salad untouched. "I was surprised by the turnout. Meredith had been telling me the whole idea was a mistake, and frankly, I thought she was right."

"You're kidding," I said. "You don't think a Bradley—any Bradley—would get involved in less than a sure thing?"

"Bruce, you mean? He may have a degree in business, but that doesn't necessarily mean he's got a head for it. I remember him as an artistic child, and I always thought his choice of a major had more to do with what Meredith wanted than with Bruce's interests. Besides, he's crazy in love and not thinking straight. Trina might be good for him— shake loose that traditional mindset he's grown up with—but I don't know. The Tea Room is clearly her domain."

"Sounds like a good partnership to me. Trina teaches the meditation classes and Bruce runs the cash register." I chased the last few green beans around my plate and finally trapped them between the fork and a chunk of cornbread.

"How many people in Jesus Creek do you think will pay for those classes? Or for whole-grain carob brownies? Last night the food was free, and people had nothing better to do than gawk at Bruce's new wife," Delia pointed out.

"I don't know," Eloise drawled. "Those Bradleys have a knack for making money."

"Marty took over his dad's lumber store—the only lumber store in the county," Delia said. "And Meredith started the only florist in town. She'd have done okay even if she hadn't had a talent for the job. Both those businesses are necessary. Everybody needs a new roof or deck or a bridal bouquet at some point."

"Oh, my Lord!" Eloise looked as if her house had just caved in. "Kay, honey! Now that Meredith's dead, what are you gonna do about your wedding flowers?"

"Huh?" Delia and I said together.

"Well, you'll never be able to get anything worth paying for out of that Benton Harbor florist!" Eloise went on. "I expect you'll have to go all the way to Nashville."

"I didn't even know you were getting married!" Delia reached across both our plates to grab my hand. "When did this come up? Why didn't you tell me?"

"Because this is the first I've heard of it." For a few seconds I considered the possibility that I'd entered the Twilight Zone, a shadowy aisle where the bride is the last to know.

"Now, you and Wayne have been together long enough. Everybody knows you're perfect for each other. It's time you set a date, but the point is, where will you get the flowers?" Eloise propped a hand on her hip and contemplated the options as her cigarette burned down.

I sighed—with relief or annoyance, I wasn't sure which. Wayne hadn't been making plans behind my back after all. The wedding was just an outgrowth of Eloise's carved-in-stone expectations.

I'd known a lot of women who got married and had children because someone else assumed they would. Most of them waited until it was far too late to think about whether the plan made sense. I counted myself among the lucky few who had figured out ahead of time that I do not enjoy the suffocating closeness of traditional family life. That is, I have no intention of devoting my life to meal planning and interior decoration that revolves around the petty desires of other people. Call me un-American, call me unnatural, but don't call me to chair the PTA bake sale.

"Eloise, wedding decorations are not a priority just now."

"Bound to be soon, though." Eloise went on as if she hadn't noticed the tight muscles in my jaw. "When are you and Wayne gonna do it?"

"Obviously not until they resolve the baby's breath dilemma. Let's see what sort of wreaths turn up at Meredith's funeral. Maybe we can all find a new florist by examining the pall and sprays." Delia was running interference for me, she being more sensitive to my mood than Eloise.

"I'm sure Meredith will be spinning in her grave," Eloise pronounced, "if anybody sends plastic roses to her funeral!"

"Poor Meredith," Delia sighed. "She was always so careful to plan ahead. If she'd only made up arrangements for her own funeral and stored them, there wouldn't be a problem."

"I'd like to point out," I said, "that in at least one other instance, Meredith's planning fell short. I guess after she turned up pregnant, she learned to be more organized."

Eloise lit a fresh cigarette and tossed her enhanced blonde hair. "Sugar, she wasn't the first. Back then, of course, the Free Love revolution had just started rolling and some of the girls just got married and didn't make any bones about it. Personally I've never seen the point of having a big church wedding with the bride sticking out to here and wearin' a white dress!"

While Eloise is in many ways a liberated woman, she just can't shake her upbringing. With a number of ex-husbands to her credit, she had been careful to wear the traditional white wedding gown for the first wedding only. She almost certainly had not been pregnant at the time—her only child was fathered by husband number three. She's never said whether she qualified for that white dress in other respects, and my upbringing didn't even allow me to think about asking.

"But Meredith did the right thing? Slunk away and put the baby up for adoption."

"Right or wrong," Eloise waffled. "At least she was discreet."

"You mean you didn't know?" I was stunned. Eloise's spy network is vast and provides her with information faster than lightning. It was inconceivable that she'd have missed a single bit of gossip.

"I was away at college," Delia said.

Talking over her, Eloise corrected me. "Well, of course I knew she was pregnant! Everybody did. But Meredith and her people kept quiet about it and everything moved right along."

I'd known when I left home that morning that I'd get more than a good meal at Eloise's. Now my hunch was about to pay off, and I fairly gloated inside while keeping an interested-yet-puzzled expression on my face.

"Gosh, Eloise," I said innocently, "you mean everybody knew Meredith had a baby? Then why were we all surprised when Vanessa showed up here?"

"There must've been some who missed it"—Eloise stared pointedly at Delia—"for one reason or another. The rest of us were polite enough all along to pretend we hadn't noticed."

Ah, yes. The Southern Way.

With the groundwork established, I started to build on it. "You mean half the town knew and kept quiet? What about the boy and his family? Didn't any of them care about keeping the baby? Didn't he even offer to marry Meredith?"

Eloise's mouth opened as if she were about to speak, but no words came out. She closed it and tried again. "You know, I don't believe the boy was from around here. As I recall, Meredith used to go off and spend summers with some cousins, and I believe it all happened there. Could be the boy never even knew."

"Surely she'd have told him!" I insisted.

"Not necessarily. Even then Meredith had an iron will. If she'd split up with him or anything like that before she found out, she never would have changed her mind. You know how that woman could carry a grudge!"

Delia was the bridge that spanned the generation gap. "It's also possible he did know and Meredith's family didn't find him suitable. Or Meredith didn't."

Both she and Eloise seemed to agree that whoever Vanessa's father was, he'd never been around Jesus Creek. It occurred to me, though, that if Vanessa had recently surprised him with her existence, he could've been mightily upset about having been kept in the dark about this important part of his life. Would he have been mad enough to kill, though?

I met German at the PD a little before three o'clock to catch up on any news he might have and to take possession of the beeper. It was one of those days when I could hardly wait to saddle up and ride. I planned to spend most of the afternoon in the woods, working Sundance into a lather and pumping my adrenaline level over the top with a series of unnecessary and dangerous stunts. Physically demanding activity is a great way to relieve tension.

German's horse, Pudding, was tied up out front, happily enjoying water and hay. Consumed by his image, German refused to call the horse by its name. Pudding, it seems, isn't macho enough for our assistant chief, so he calls the beautiful paint Comanche. I don't suppose Pudding minds, but it gives you an idea of how impossible German is, doesn't it? Worse still, German refuses to use the English saddle that comes with the package. When Rhonda told him she didn't have anything with a saddle horn, German went out and bought his own. It's covered in turquoise and silver and I don't know what else. It might look impressive if German knew the first thing about riding, but Rhonda's instruction had gone in one of German's ears and right through his empty head. He slouches along on the poor horse's back with elbows flying until I just want to scream at him, "Get a clue!"

He won't wear a helmet, either, clinging valiantly to a Stetson he bought on his honeymoon in Texas. I suppose his hard head won't suffer much damage if he takes a spill.

"Nothing!" he said, in response to my query about clues in the Bradley case. By the time I'd completed my report to Agent Warner it had been far too late to go knocking on doors and waking people, so I'd left the legwork for German. He was probably mad about that.

"Not a blessed thing!" he went on. "At least, that's what Agent Warner says. He's so tight-lipped, I'm surprised he hadn't starved to death by now."

"Maybe he really doesn't know anything yet." I was defending the enemy only because I like to watch German's face turn red. "I'll give him a call this evening and try to pry him loose."

German grunted. It's his first language.

"Did you talk to Meredith's neighbors? Did anybody see anything?"

German rolled his eyes at me. "Yes, I've been out all morning doing my job, and no, nobody saw a thing." His mood had been rotten ever since Chief Gassler went on vacation and left him in charge. Ordinarily I'd have snapped right back at him, but that day I was feeling sorry for poor German, who was facing the pressure of a murder investigation.

I tried a little levity to brighten his day. "Was Bernie able to salvage anything from that spaceship? Find any survivors?"

Al, our day-shift dispatcher, chuckled. "You know how sneaky those aliens are. They turned on the cloaking device and Bernie wasn't able to see the ship."

"Gee, you'd think something that big would make a helluva dent in the woods where it went down. Bernie didn't find any crushed trees, either?"

"Told ya the aliens were sneaky," Al said.

"If you two are finished?" German slapped the beeper down on Al's desk and handed me a file folder. "That's my notes on the Bradley case. I had a long talk with Bruce and the rest of them this morning, not to mention the blind and deaf neighbors, and everything's there in writing." This was German's way of suggesting that I write up my own report and add it to the file.

I patted my left shirt pocket where my notepad resides. "It's all here. I'll write it up now."

German fiddled around in the office a few more minutes, probably making sure I really did intend to file my report. Little did he know that I was happy to complete that chore. I wanted all the strings knotted so I could cut loose on Sundance and enjoy a few hours on the trail.

First I read German's report, carefully studying what the Bradleys' neighbors had had to say. None of them had noticed anything unusual until they saw me arrive. After that, they'd apparently been watching through the curtains, because every single one of them reported with amazing accuracy every step I'd taken, and they'd given full and accurate descriptions of Mark Warner and his team. If only that curiosity had gone into play earlier in the evening.

The PD has a snazzy computer, but the typewriter is still in the office, tucked into a dark corner where it sits patiently waiting for me to type up a report. I'd as soon do it in longhand, but the spaces provided on the forms are just the right size to hold half a cursive word or three typewritten ones. Since I often have a great deal to say, I need the old Royal to get my point across.

There's not much room for originality either.

Officer Martin arrived at the scene at 9:12 P.M. No one wants atmosphere-rich details, such as that I was stunned and sickened by what I'd found at the Bradley house.

I was tempted to write *Officer Martin opined that the Bradley family should have been allowed to enjoy their happy evening without the intrusion of some scumbag criminal's actions.*

It is important to note every fact on these reports, and omission of a single word can make one look a fool when it goes to court and the attorneys start ripping a testimony to bits. Dr. Daryl James examined the victim's body, I typed, and did not add his comment about vampires.

It took quite a long time to finish my report, as I am careful to make it as detailed and boring as possible. That way, when the attorneys read through it, it hurts them as much as it does me.

If I'd only typed a little faster, I could have been long gone before Mrs. Jackson and her herd of grandchildren descended upon the PD. Life is full of that—opportunities and risks that you aren't even aware you've missed. Tractors that poke along in front of your car because a guardian angel wants to keep you from getting to the intersection at just the moment some drunk runs the stop sign, for instance. Mrs. Jackson didn't seem like a blessing at the time, but perhaps those twenty minutes I spent listening to her were the very ones in which Sundance or I would have been shot by an out-of-season hunter, like that game warden who died a while back.

"I want to report a missing person," she said plainly, as the oldest of the three grandchildren chased the other two around and around Al's desk.

"Oh?" I said, pulling a legal pad from a drawer and sliding my chair up beside the desk. The children swerved around me and continued to run, squealing as they went.

Mrs. Jackson was distraught and totally oblivious to the look of pained concern on Al's face. "It's my daughter, Jen. Jennifer Atwater, she is now."

"Yes," I said. "I know Jen. We were in school together. Uh . . . are any of these hers?" I indicated the little darlings racing around the room.

"They're all hers!" Mrs. Jackson said with more than a trace of exasperation. "I expected so much more from her. Jen was an awful pretty girl, you know. And smart, too. I always told her she could be somebody special, but she took up with that Billy Atwater and next thing you know, she had to get married. It about broke my heart."

Mrs. Jackson seemed more angry than heart-broken, and she still did not feel compelled to quiet Jen's angels. Al hunkered protectively over his computer.

"And who is it that's missing, ma'am?"

"Well, it's Jen, of course!" She said this as if I were dim to think that anyone else on earth could be the cause of her anguish.

"Oh, I see." I wrote Jen's full name on the legal pad. "When did you see her last, Mrs. Jackson?"

"I hadn' seen her since one day last week, but she's only been missing since last night. That Billy dropped all these young'uns off at my place this morning. He said Jen took the car last night and went to the Qwik Stop over in Benton Harbor for a gallon of milk. She's still not back."

The smallest child, who looked to be about two, stumbled and fell. He shrieked his displeasure as his siblings hopped over him and continued the chase.

How could I explain to Mrs. Jackson that Jen wasn't missing, but had simply and understandably run away from home? "She's been gone only a few hours, then?"

"That's right. And I know from watching TV that you can't start looking for her yet, but I want it on record that that Billy Atwater did something to my Jen and he's not gettin' away with it!"

"Actually, Mrs. Jackson, it's the federal authorities who don't start an investigation on a missing person for forty-eight hours. We can start any time we like, and I'll certainly get right to work on this." I try to be a helpful public servant, cheerful, obedient, and loyal. Or is that a wife?

"Has Billy hurt Jen in the past?" I asked.

"He most surely has! He hurt every chance she ever had when he married her!" Mrs. Jackson reached out with one arm and grabbed the towhead just rounding the corner. The other children went about their business undeterred. With remarkable lack of interest in maintaining discipline, Mrs. Jackson dropped her hand and set free the seething ball of energy.

"Have you checked with Jen's friends and other family members?"

"What do you think I've been doing all morning?"

My eyes jumped involuntarily to the bulletin board where a game of Jump-and-Grab had erupted. "I'll tell you what, ma'am," I said. "I'll keep an eye out for Jen this evening, and you let me know if you hear from her. If she's not back home by tomorrow night, give us a call and we'll file an official missing person report. Okay?" Jen's mother gave me a description of her daughter, along with a two-year-old snapshot featuring Jen and a newborn child. It wasn't an artistic picture—the focus was fuzzy and the top inch or so of Jen's head was missing—but even in two dimensions, I could recognize the placid nature that I'd always associated with Jen.

She'd always been pretty, but without the energy and perkiness associated with youth, Jen often disappeared into her surroundings. She'd been sweet and calm, with acceptable grades and a habit of taking on the dirty work within the few school clubs she'd joined.

Thinking about it with that snapshot in my hand, I realized that Jen had never quite fit into any of the cliques that existed back then. She wasn't cool, she wasn't sophisticated, she wasn't smart or wild or athletic. She'd always been Jen, the girl everyone liked just fine and then forgot about as soon as she was out of sight. If she'd tried to disappear into the crowd, she couldn't have done a better job. Maybe this was the inevitable outcome—maybe Jen had run away to a hidden community of blandness, where she fit in perfectly.

Apparently she'd found a temporary niche with Billy Atwater, though. There'd been no domestic disputes, no rumors of trouble within the marriage, and no complaints from Jen herself. At least, none that I was aware of. I saw her once or twice a week, shopping in town or just out walking with one or more children in tow, and she'd always seemed as calm and self-contained as a Buddha.

I should watch for a '74 tan Chevy, Mrs. Jackson told me, with a gray-primered passenger door. She felt that Jen should have been driving a slightly more impressive vehicle, but "that Billy Atwater" was too tight-fisted to buy it for her. I did not mention that Billy's gas station mechanic salary probably didn't allow room in the budget for a Porsche.

Al was a trembling wreck by the time we cleared the office, so I took it upon myself to retrieve notes and pushpins that had been ripped off the bulletin board. I felt as if I'd put in a full shift already, and this strengthened my resolve to fight off any lingering urges for marital conformity. If only Jen had followed her mother's dream, she might have become "something special," instead of a statistic.

CHAPTER 5

BY THE TIME I'D WALKED DOWN TO THE small pasture where the PD horses stay, snared Sundance and saddled him, I was sweaty and irritable. I don't like days that begin with bad news. It seems to me that's an omen, or a curse, that warns me to beware until the sun sets and rises again. The only thing that could make me feel better, I decided, would be a hard ride through the woods west of town.

We clip-clopped down the street, soaking in the laziness of a hot summer Sunday. Proctor's Gas Station was closed, and I was not inclined to ride along the highway for several miles to catch Billy Atwater at home. My guess was that Jen would be back in her rightful place by bedtime, and I saw no point in wasting half the afternoon on her mother's hysterical allegations. Some people attract adventure and excitement, and some lead mediocre lives. Jen was definitely among the latter, and I doubted very much that she'd been dragged away at gunpoint by South American drug lords.

Traffic was almost nonexistent, which is normal for that time of day. It would pick up in another hour or so as folks drove their air-conditioned cars to evening services. Some hardy souls who worship at the in-town churches would travel on foot, maybe leaving home a little early in order to visit with neighbors along the way. All in all, Sunday evening is a pleasant time, even with August beating down upon us, trying its best to break our spirits. Maybe it's this little taste of eternal furnaces that encourages the spiritually lax to get out and worship on a day when sipping ice tea under the air conditioner would be far easier.

Down at the memorial park, the two new picnic tables were covered with white paper cloths, left over from the community potluck that had just ended. After morning services a goodly crowd would enjoy dinner on the grounds, sharing their news and ideas the way good neighbors should. Mayor Mooten instigated that as part of his Simpler Times program. Throughout his campaign, Henry Mooten had stressed the importance of regaining the values of our forebears. Since the only other candidate spent the majority of his time out-of-state, and since he had no definable platform anyway, most everybody supported Henry in his sincere effort to restore an honest, peaceful, wholesome environment for us all.

There'd been a surprisingly supportive response to the new mayor's ideas, and all sorts of volunteer groups had sprung up—the Committee to Study the History of Jesus Creek, the Beautification Committee, the Panel for Organization of Family Events. All worthy causes, and they kept folks busy and out of trouble.

Marty and Meredith Bradley had usually attended the potluck, I recalled. In fact, it was on one of the

rare occasions I'd been there that Meredith had told
me about, and introduced me to, Vanessa. I'd come
along late, having originally planned to spend a
happy evening at home with Wayne, but then he'd
called to say he'd be working late. Not being of a
mind that day to spend a lonely time with reruns and
a bologna sandwich, I'd ordered a chocolate pie from
the diner, put on a clean pair of jeans, and walked
down the street to join my neighbors in a communal
feast. I'd actually enjoyed it, and couldn't remember
why I hadn't attended again since.

As I recalled, Meredith had presented Vanessa to
me with no particular emotion—neither joy nor
embarrassment—and had shortly thereafter wandered away to discuss with Eloise the possibility of
daily fresh flowers for the diner tables. The plastic
roses were still holding their own between salt and
pepper, so Meredith's sales pitch obviously hadn't
swayed Eloise.

Vanessa and I had spent a few awkward moments
struggling with the stilted conversation that always
results when two strangers with nothing in common
are forced together. I'd asked her how she liked
Jesus Creek, she'd been noncommittal and we'd
moved on to the riveting topic of weather trends
before Meredith whisked her daughter away for
another introduction.

As I proceeded down the street, I spotted Trina
and Vanessa saying their goodbyes to Mrs.
Lambdin. Each of them had a small suitcase. I
found that sufficiently interesting to nudge Sundance into a more lively walk, which took us to the

front of Mrs. Lambdin's yard just as Vanessa and Trina stepped onto the sidewalk.

"Are you on foot in this heat?" I asked them.

"The car's down by the Tea Room," Trina answered me. She set her suitcase on the concrete, implying that she was willing to stop and chat awhile. "We have to clean up down there, and take Minerva home. It doesn't look as if we'll be at the Tea Room for a while. . . ."

To show that I was feeling equally sociable, I dismounted and hitched Sundance to the rusting wrought-iron fence that surrounded the Lambdin yard. "Sun is ready for a break," I said, in case they'd missed my intent. "When he doesn't get his way, he pouts like a two-year-old."

"What a sweetheart!" Trina said. Putting down her purse, she made a beeline for my horse. Vanessa, seeing that they wouldn't be moving for a while, lowered a small bag but remained in her spot, warily watching Trina with Sundance.

"Am I allowed to play with him while he's on duty?" Trina asked, already stroking Sun's nose.

"Go ahead," I told her. "But protect your chest. He likes to bite, uh, women."

"Oh, no!" Trina squealed in a baby-talk voice. "Are you a naughty boy?"

I left Sundance in Trina's adoring hands while I joined Vanessa. "I guess you'll be staying at Bruce and Trina's for a while yet."

Vanessa looked at the overnight bag at her feet, then back up at me. "For a while. I had to borrow some clothes from a couple of women at church.

Everything I have is in the house, and Trina's clothes sure don't fit."

Vanessa was at least six inches taller than her sister-in-law, and even if she'd been willing to wear too-short dresses, her large-boned figure couldn't have squeezed into Trina's dainty outfits.

"Are you okay? How's Bruce handling it?" I felt as if I needed to avoid the harsh words like death, even with Vanessa. While technically part of the family, she still seemed to me to be a very distant relation to the Bradleys, and therefore a comfortable source of information about them.

"Trina and I had to talk Marty into staying at their place. He kept insisting he'd go home. Finally we made him understand that the police have closed off the house. I suppose it's normal for him to be confused, under the circumstances." A slight frown was the only indication that this upset affected her in any way.

I could read sincerity on her face, but her eyes were still slightly glazed—unfocused, like they'd been the night before. "How's your headache?" I asked.

"Easing. Normally I'd let the Demerol get me through it, but today . . . well, it didn't seem fair that I should go off to sleep while the others are hurting so much."

I didn't want to sell her short, but it seemed to me that Vanessa's sympathy for the family was the only emotion behind those beautiful slurry eyes. She hadn't mentioned her own loss. She hadn't mentioned the tragedy of a fine and talented woman's death, either.

"Must be doubly hard on you," I ventured, "losing your mother before you even got a chance to know her well."

Vanessa half smiled and watched her fingers play with each other. "It's ironic, isn't it? Maybe it wasn't meant for me to get close to Meredith. At least I've still got my real mother." She turned her head to see what I thought of that. "The mother who did all the work. That's the real one, isn't it? I mean, Meredith could have been a test tube."

I was stunned by her callous comparison, and she seemed to understand that. Rather than backtracking or trying to explain further, Vanessa gave me a sweet, tolerant smile of the sort that Mother Teresa might bestow upon an ignorant sinner who had failed to grasp a simple principle of doctrine.

"I'll always be grateful to Meredith, of course. She gave me life and a good family. I'm glad I told her that. We managed to have some very productive conversation, in spite of our awkwardness with each other."

I wondered if she'd mentioned test tubes to Meredith. One thing was certain—Vanessa had inherited Meredith's habit of speaking plainly! Perhaps that's what she'd meant by *productive*, though. Those two wouldn't have held back or wasted time on small talk.

Trina looked over at Vanessa with a startled expression, gave Sundance one last pat on his neck, and started toward us. She looked like a resident from Henry's ideal village in her long dark skirt and simple cotton blouse. Her hair was tucked into a chignon, but instead of looking dowdy, it gave Trina an exotic flavor. I was glad I'd kept my riding helmet on and my own shaggy, short hair covered.

"Are you tired, Vanessa?" she asked. "Maybe we should go home and put you to bed."

"No," Vanessa said bluntly. "I told you, I'd rather carry my weight."

How odd that Vanessa viewed mourning as a chore to be done. Trina must have realized that her sister-in-law's comments were inappropriate, for she jumped in to smooth the ruffled edges.

"Vannie has such a clear understanding," she said to me. "I know with my head that death and grief are natural and necessary parts of the life process. Still, my heart can't accept that. I've reminded myself so many times today that Meredith's passing is a blessing for her. She's moved on to a higher level and I envy her that. If only Bruce and Marty didn't have to suffer . . . but that's a learning experience for them, too."

Trina's theory wasn't new, nor was it startling. I'd wondered myself why people fear and struggle against death when almost every belief system promises joy and blessings in the afterlife. Of course, not too many years before, I'd put up a mighty battle against death myself, and the thought of harps and heavenly rewards hadn't entered my mind at the time.

"You were all closer to her," Vanessa said. "I barely knew Meredith, so her death isn't likely to affect me in the same way. I barely know any of you, come to that."

I wondered if Vanessa realized how cold those remarks made her seem. Hadn't anyone told her she was a suspect in her mother's murder? Or didn't the Bradleys realize it either? I ought to warn them, I thought. They need to start thinking about how to proceed. The cop in me, though, grabbed my tongue and wouldn't let go.

"Did the TBI come out and talk to you last night?" I asked. I was careful to direct my question to the air and not to Vanessa directly.

Both of them nodded. "They insisted on taking blood from all of us. For comparison, they said. And they weren't very considerate of Bruce and Marty," Trina complained. There was a steel edge behind those words, hinting at the kind of core inside that serene, willowy woman. If her Tea Room supplies included voodoo devices, I predicted that Mark Warner would soon be developing an unpleasant skin condition.

"They don't try very hard," I agreed. "Then again, time wasted on pleasantries is time wasted, and we all want them to spend every minute working on the case."

"You're investigating, too, aren't you?" Trina asked eagerly.

"Yes, but we're limited in what we can do. Most small-town police are short on money and equipment. And personnel. This new mobile unit has turned out to be a brilliant idea. Some of us get our noses out of joint"—I grinned an admission of guilt—"but by and large we're all better off this way."

Trina was not persuaded. "They don't have to be quite so rude, do they? I'd think a personal approach would be more effective."

"Sometimes it is. And other times it's a draw-back. If we're too close to a victim or a suspect, it blinds us. When a friend is involved, for instance, it's hard to remain objective." Were they listening to me at all?

Vanessa looked at her watch and stiffened slightly. "We need to go. I still have to get a shower before church."

"Wouldn't you rather stay home tonight?" Trina urged. "Between your headache and the stress—"

"Being in church is the best thing for stress," Vanessa announced. "I felt a lot better after this morning's service. It's always cooler in church than anywhere else. There's a kind of peacefulness you don't find anywhere else, not even in your own room."

Trina sighed, resigned. "Then we'll go. I don't want to leave the boys alone too long. Give me your bag and I'll carry it."

Vanessa hefted the small suitcase easily and hung it from her shoulder. "I can carry it, Trina," she said, leaving no room for argument. "There's really too much here anyway. Half these clothes would have done me. I only wish I could get my quilting out of the house."

"You quilt?" I asked. I don't know why I was sur-prised. Lots of young people do, but it will always be an old lady's hobby to me. Probably has something to do with early memories of my grandmothers working at their frames, those little needles going endlessly in and out of the quilt.

"Vanessa not only makes quilts," Trina informed me, "she designs her own patterns. It's an amazing talent, if you ask me. You should see some of the ones she's created."

"I was just about to start piecing one for Meredith," Vanessa said. Suddenly, and for the first time, I saw life in her eyes.

I remembered the box of fabric I'd seen in her closet—the subtly different grays and blues, with a deep red swatch on top—the color of Meredith's skin in death, and the blood that stood out so vividly against it.

"Vannie makes terribly profound connections between quilts and life," Trina said, beaming. "Which one is she?"

Not in the least annoyed at being asked to perform, Vanessa studied me intently for a minute, then said, "Drunkard's Path."

Trina and I both looked at her with a complete lack of comprehension. Vanessa sighed, obviously frustrated by our thickness.

"That pattern looks frenzied," she complained. "The path wanders here and there, shooting out points. Kay is that sort of person—wandering from one place in her life to another, popping off now and then to look at a weed or something growing beside the trail."

Perhaps I was being too sensitive, but I felt I'd been insulted. Trina, on the other hand, was absolutely ecstatic.

"Isn't that marvelous, Kay?"

"I'm not sure," I said, "that I like being called a Drunkard's Path."

"You're definitely not straight lines and Amish colors," Vanessa told me. "You're more complicated than that. If I quilted you, I'd use mostly prints, with just one solid to represent your unwavering idealism."

"My what?" Where on earth did she get that? "I'm not idealistic. I'm a cop."

Vanessa almost smiled. "The good guys are always idealists. The bad guys aren't blinded by dreams of a better world, and they certainly don't work to improve conditions for anyone else."

I had to give her that one, but I still thought she'd jumped to conclusions about my personality. If Trina had any thoughts of pulling Vanessa into the Tea Room and offering quilt readings, I predicted that customers would disappear quickly.

"I'm a Double Irish Chain," Trina said proudly. She looked to Vanessa for the explanation.

"Trina's pattern looks very simple at first glance, just squares and rectangles. It's actually very complex. It winds and weaves into a tangle that won't let your eye move away."

If Trina found that flattering, then she wasn't listening closely. I consoled myself with the thought that, at least, a Drunkard's Path wasn't as conniving as a Double Irish Chain.

Bored with the game, Vanessa picked up her suitcase and started down the sidewalk. "I'm going on to the Tea Room," she said.

I put a restraining hand on Trina's arm. "Let's talk about Vanessa," I said once she was out of earshot. "She doesn't seem all that upset about Meredith's death." I'd decided the time for soft soap had passed.

A small trench formed between Trina's eyes and I

noticed a fine sheen of perspiration above her lip. "That painkiller has numbed her. If you think about it, she's just like Mere. No nonsense, straight to the heart."

Right where the spindle got Meredith, I could have said. I didn't, of course.

Trina shooed away a honeybee that had been buzzing near her shoulder, probably attracted to the herbal scent she wore. "She's very strong. I think she might have been Joan of Arc in a previous life. Don't you think Vannie could lead an army?"

"A woman who knows the difference in lumber grade could do anything."

Trina laughed her wind-chime laugh, and I had the idea it was the first time all day she'd been without the weight of grief. I was glad I could give her that, if only for a moment. Suddenly the tiny woman felt like a friend; I admired her fierce loyalty to her husband and his family, and I was sure she'd go to bat for any innocent victim with the degree of passion and determination it takes to keep goodness alive in this world.

"Really, though," she said. "Vanessa is special. She has a kind of strength I've never seen in anyone else. And she has a spiritual glow that astounds me. Every now and then I catch it—there's a change in her face, almost like she's seen the far edge of the universe and understands it." Trina looked at me, wanting to be sure I understood.

"Trina, have any of you talked to a lawyer?" I asked. "Delia said she'd suggested someone."

"About the will, you mean? Meredith had that

changed a few weeks ago. I checked with Mr. Maddox and everything is in order."

I hadn't been talking about a will, but her mention of it snapped me to attention. "Why did she change her will, Trina?" I asked carefully.

"To include Vanessa. It's a good thing Meredith was conscientious about those things, isn't it? Not that Marty and Bruce wouldn't have made sure Vanessa was included."

"Trina, listen to me. It's very important that you talk to a lawyer. Today, if possible. Vanessa could be in really big trouble."

I could almost hear the lid snap shut, and I swear Trina's eyes narrowed the way Bella's do just before she scratches the fire out of me. "Are you going to arrest Vannie?" she asked coldly.

"I've barely investigated, Trina. The TBI is going at it fast and furious, and you must realize that Vanessa is the prime suspect."

Her mouth tilted upward without the cooperation of the rest of her face. "But you know her, Kay. Vannie wouldn't kill anyone. You'll have to make them understand."

And with that, she retrieved the little suitcase and was gone. In spite of her casual air, I knew she was distracted. She didn't even notice Sundance as she hurried past him.

Poor Sundance must have thought he'd been commandeered by a madwoman bent on destroying both horse and rider. I put him into a canter as soon as we hit the trail, and the more I dodged, ducked, and dived to avoid tree branches and ground ruts, the faster I wanted to go. Not even fallen trees could stop me—I just grabbed mane and urged Sun to jump, scaring myself half to death every time, but determined to keep going until I collapsed. If my beeper had gone off, I might well have ignored my sworn duty in favor of meeting my soul's needs.

If I passed the UFO crash site, I didn't notice. Neither did Sundance, but it would take more than an extraterrestrial presence to spook him. The only time he's shied away from anything was during the Fourth of July parade when Miss Constance Winter's balloon-and-streamer-adorned wheelchair rolled backward and out of control on a downhill run and was headed straight for our mounted escort at the end of the parade. Fortunately, a quick-thinking citizen was able to grab the chair and prevent catastrophe.

By the time I felt easy enough to slow to a reasonable speed, Sun was lathered and panting. I took pity on him and dismounted, letting Sun drink and soak his feet at the first creek we came to. I spent the time rubbing gluey spiderwebs off my face and arms. I don't know how they measure it, but every spider in Angela County builds its trap at just the right height to catch me when I'm atop my horse.

Those who'd been in the right place at the right time to see him had said that Jason wore a bike helmet with full-face visor. Every time a web smacked me in the face, I cursed Jason and wished him into a nest of seed ticks.

While Sundance sucked water, I looked around the dense foliage and scrub brush, wondering where in these woods Jason hid out. I knew he was out there somewhere, laughing at us and plotting his next disruptive incursion into Jesus Creek. Every witness to his numerous escapes reported that he'd headed into or toward the woods. He couldn't have chosen better concealment anywhere. I looked ahead and to both sides, and saw no more than a few feet beyond myself. If Jason wore drab clothing and stood still, he could've been right beside me and I wouldn't have spotted him. Just in case, I stuck out my tongue.

The trail was quieter as I rode back to town, without the roar of wind passing by my head. We kept up a brisk walk and I was able to ward off spiderwebs with a leafy branch I'd broken off a slim maple. At the same time, I watched the ground for signs of tire tracks, hoping for a lucky break that would lead me to Jason.

When we came out of the woods at the edge of town, I spotted a dust-covered Chevy rattling down Primrose Lane. I couldn't tell its natural color for the layers of mud, but I was reasonably sure it wasn't Jen Atwater's. I wondered if she'd made it home yet. As far as I knew, Jen did not routinely disappear, but who could tell? After all, her husband was the person most likely to have noticed her absence, and he hadn't complained.

It seemed to me that Mrs. Jackson might have jumped the gun in reporting her daughter's disappearance. Or maybe she just wanted those kids taken off her hands, and who could blame her? I decided that I'd go by Proctor's Gas Station the next day and talk to Billy Atwater, assuming Jen could still be considered a missing person by then.

Two dozen cars were parked in front of the Baptist church, their windows wide open to allow any stray breeze to come through. At seven P.M., the sun was only a little more forgiving than at noon, and I found one more reason to be thankful for my four-legged transportation—no stale heat trapped inside when you're riding a convertible.

At the far end of the row of cars, I spied a reedy figure tucking flyers inside the open cars. Once or twice, when the windows were closed, he'd put the white paper under the windshield wiper.

"What's this?" I said to Sundance. We headed toward the advertiser, who had suddenly disappeared beyond the last car in the line.

My heart threatened to choke me when I heard the distinctive rumble of a motorcycle engine. Better still, I saw it! It shot out into the street and headed south on Primrose at a leisurely speed.

I asked Sundance for a gallop, but he evidently figured he'd had his workout for the day. He moved along at a brisk trot when I insisted, but adamantly refused to pick up speed.

"And to think I was just congratulating myself on having a horse instead of a car!" I told him with disgust.

Sundance perked up his ears for a second, then decided I wasn't saying anything important.

"Look at that, you dumb critter!"

Sundance came to a halt as the motorcycle sped away into the distance.

I made it to the ground in two seconds, without giving Sun the usual good-boy affection. Tugging on

the reins, I led him beside the nearest car and
ripped the flyer off its windshield.

BROTHERHOOD OF STRENGTH, it read.

For too long we have allowed foreign minds to
dictate our way of life! Where has it gotten us?
Women are leaving their homes and children to
go out and take jobs away from men who need
them!

Jobs and civil rights are being taken away from
men who have earned them and given to foreigners
and others who want to destroy the American way
of life!

The Time Has Come
for honest men to take back what is rightfully
theirs!

Think About It!

CHAPTER 6

THE CHURCH DOORS OPENED AND SPEWED forth a congregation renewed in their faith and spiritual strength. Faces reflected the serenity of souls confident of the guidance and protection of a higher power.

The expression on *my* face set me apart immediately. I was baffled and perturbed by the claims made in print by this Brotherhood of Strength, and perhaps a bit unnerved. As the Sunday night worshipers swarmed around me and gradually dispersed, I stopped a few people at random to ask about the flyers.

"Sheesh! Again?" Clay Griffith said. "I found one of these things stuck on my front door this morning."

"What is it?" Mrs. Griffith asked. She took the flyer from his hand and scanned it.

Her husband snorted. "Probably somebody trying to sell us a credit card."

"Do you mind if I keep this?" I asked.

A half-dozen hands thrust their flyers at me and I collected them all. "Thanks, guys. Any of you know what this Brotherhood of Strength is about? There's nothing on here about how to contact them if you want to join."

"Is it a religious sect? Odd that they'd spread these around during another church's service." Vanessa's voice came from directly behind me.

She wore a simple, shapeless cotton dress, beige with scattered blue flowers. From the look of it, Vanessa had gotten the dregs of Mrs. Lambdin's closet.

"It doesn't mention religion," I said after another quick read-through. "Worshipers of the All Powerful Male, maybe."

All of the women in the group around me snickered and a few men grinned. "Where do I sign up?" Jerry Bottoms asked. "I've been trying to get Janet to worship me for years."

"Dream on," his wife said, but gazed adoringly at him.

"If any of you learn more about this, let me know, will you?"

As the group dispersed and headed toward their cars and homes, they called out promises of compliance. In just a few minutes Vanessa, Marty, Sundance, and I were the only proof of life in Jesus Creek.

"It's true, I guess. Small towns really do roll up the sidewalks after dark." Vanessa looked around at the suddenly deserted street.

"We take spells," I told her. "Mostly nothing happens, but from time to time every nut in town goes on a tangent. I hate when that happens, and by the look of it, I'm going to be in a bad mood for a while."

Vanessa actually smiled, and her normally bland

face was transformed. For the first time I saw behind the somber, serious woman to the fun-loving child. "If you ask Trina, she might be able to do an astrological chart that would show you when to expect these uprisings. You could plan your vacation around it."

It was worth a try, I figured. "Has she done a chart for you?" And did it hint at the trouble you're in? I wondered.

"She tried. Actually, she isn't very good at astrology. Trina gets emotionally involved with her charts. She slants them to reflect what she sees in a person, so if she knows you—"

"The stars in her eyes blind her to the stars in the sky?"

"Something like that. She means well."

Marty was dressed in his summer-casual Sunday-go-to-meeting clothes—dress pants and a short-sleeve shirt with discreet necktie. His healthy tan had paled overnight, it seemed. "Trina surprises us every day," he said.

I was touched by his effort to join in the conversation. It took tremendous courage to get Marty out into the world at all; he certainly didn't have to be sociable. If the preacher had chosen his topic carefully, the evening's sermon might have contributed to Marty's coping ability. Apparently Vanessa wasn't the only member of the family who found the church comforting.

"Are they picking us up or should we walk?" Vanessa asked.

Marty looked at his watch, then glanced down the street. "Bruce said he'd be here. Maybe they lost track of the time. Trina wanted him to help her unpack some boxes. She's probably just trying to keep him busy, though."

"Here they are," Vanessa said, spying a pair of headlights coming down the street.

She let the conversation drop as Bruce's car pulled up to the curb.

I led Sundance closer and leaned toward the driver's window as Vanessa and Marty got into the car. I could hear Bruce apologizing to them for his tardiness, and Marty and Vanessa assuring him it didn't matter a bit. Then Bruce turned to me. "Can you follow us home?" he asked. His eyes looked darker in the setting sunlight.

"Sure, Bruce. Is there a problem?"

"Yeah, I think there is." He was eager to get back, so I didn't ask for more details. Whatever he wanted, it wouldn't be frivolous—if Bruce thought I needed to ride all the way out to his house, it would be worth the trip.

"Okay. I'll be there in a couple of minutes." I hoisted myself into the saddle and set off at a trot, watching Bruce's taillights ahead of me. He was driving slower than necessary, either to keep sight of me or because he needed the extra time to fill his family in on the details of the possible problem.

I rode the two or so miles to Bruce and Trina's little white house, wondering what was up, but as soon as I reached their yard, I knew why Bruce had wanted me to see for myself.

Trina was trampling the flower bed under the front window as she nailed scrap plywood over the shattered glass. I tied Sundance to the only tree and joined them at the house.

"How'd it happen?" I asked.

"Someone threw a brick through it," Marty said tersely. "With a note."

I watched Bruce take one final nail from his wife and pound it into the board. Satisfied with the sturdiness of his work, he put an arm around Trina and the two of them came over to join the rest of us. I could see that Trina had been crying.

"Did you see who did it?"

They both shook their heads, stunned and hurt. Vanessa watched them for a moment, assessing the emotional state of her family, then marched across the yard and into the house. As if on orders, the rest of us followed her.

Bruce and Trina had been in the little rental house only a few weeks, but it already felt like a home. The front door led us into a small living room that smelled of incense and scented candles. Overstuffed furniture covered with fringed shawls made the room feel close and warm in spite of the air conditioner blowing its hardest. Colorful prints that had clearly been chosen by someone with eclectic tastes added to the homey jumble of images. I fought down my urge to inspect the titles on the bookshelves and followed the rest of them through to the kitchen.

The entire house could have fit inside Meredith's flower shop, and no effort had been made to disguise its dimensions. The kitchen allowed only enough room for a breakfast table for two, yet the younger Bradleys had managed to shove in a full-size maple dining table, and they'd surrounded that with six mismatched chairs. Candles in assorted shapes, sizes, and colors clustered to create a centerpiece. Probably short on storage space, Bruce and Trina had their battered pots and pans hanging from wall hooks, and their china stacked on open shelves above the sink.

A claustrophobe would have run screaming from the threat of suffocation, but I was enchanted by the unpretentious decor. "I love this place!" I said, and helped myself to a ladderback chair.

"You've done it now!" Bruce said with mock horror. "Trina will be inviting you over for dinner every night. She's always trying to see how many guests she can cram in here." He gave her an encouraging squeeze that seemed to improve her spirits.

"Sorry about the negative energy. The last twenty-four hours have been such a drain." Trina tucked herself into one of the chairs and pulled her knees up until she could wrap her arms around them.

I didn't doubt that. I'd seen for myself how she took on responsibility for her husband and his family. Trina would have gone without food, water, or sleep in order to tend to them. If she thought it would help, she'd have siphoned her own blood and donated it to the others. I recognized the symptoms—I used to be the same way.

"Fill me in about the window." I wanted to get right to it, before Trina suggested a group hug for healing. "When did it happen?"

Vanessa had already taken her place to my right, and now Bruce and Marty joined us at the charm-

ingly worn table. They pulled out chairs and
squeezed into them, reducing the available floor
space to about one square foot. Marty had eased
himself down slowly and carefully, as if his body
might break. Suddenly, fun-loving Marty, who could
fix almost anything until it was like new, was a
broken man.

"I guess it was about an hour ago," Bruce said.
"We were in here, going over plans for—" He broke
off, with a concerned glance at his father.

Marty filled in the words. "They were planning
Meredith's funeral. It's not fair that the kids should
have to do it, but I just can't bring myself—"

"Some people have asked about charitable donations instead of flowers," Bruce said. "Little questions take on great importance at times like this.
There's no reason Dad should have to deal with it,
though."

Bruce and Trina, on either side of Marty, reached
to take his hands. "We heard the glass break,"
Bruce went on. "And when we went into the living
room to see what had happened, we found a brick on
the floor."

"Was this after you left for church?" I asked
Vanessa and Marty.

"Yes," Trina said. "Probably right in the middle of
the service."

Vanessa wasn't annoyed that Trina spoke for her,
but I was beginning to suspect a lioness lived inside
the delicate new age goddess. She'd jumped in right
away, establishing an alibi for Vanessa and chal-
lenging me with the spark in her eyes. I'd had no
intention of blaming Vanessa for the vandalism—I'd

only wanted to get all the facts straight and jotted down—but I understood why the Bradleys were sensitive to my questions. Clearly I was in the enemy camp.

"I'll need to see the brick. And the note," I said, wanting to move on quickly before I jangled any more nerves.

Bruce reached behind him and retrieved both from the kitchen counter. He set them gingerly on the table in front of me, then folded his hands like a schoolboy waiting for his final grade.

I studied the porous red rock and knew that if it had ever held retrievable prints, that moment had passed. When a hard projectile flies into your home, instinct demands that you pick it up and fondle it. Nevertheless, I'd bag it for future reference.

Ditto the note. It had been removed from the brick, opened, spread out, and handled. I squinted to read it in the dim light from the overhead. More will die, it promised.

"Any ideas at all?" I asked.

Bruce sighed. "It had to be someone really sick. Someone who enjoys hurting others."

"A troubled soul," Trina agreed. "It's important to remember that whoever did this isn't aiming at us personally. There's a lot of pain drifting in the world and it has to go somewhere."

I wasn't at all sure that was correct. Coming on top of Meredith's death, it would have taken a coincidence of monumental proportion to fire off a random missile and have it just happen to strike the Bradleys.

I was about to gather the evidence and go, but the

ringing telephone halted my farewells. Marty turned in his chair—he being the one directly in front of the wall phone—and we all waited politely while he talked.

I spent the next few seconds surreptitiously studying Vanessa. It seemed to me her eyes had moved away from her body and were looking at some other world. Her fingers on the table moved almost imperceptibly, as if stitching a minute quilt.

There was no indication that the call had been anything other than a wrong number until Marty insisted on walking me not just to the door, but all the way to the yard. When I promised him I'd make it back to the horse on my own, he gave me a meaningful look and closed the door firmly behind us. Taking my arm in gentlemanly fashion, he led me to the tree at the street's edge where Sundance waited.

"That was more than a wrong number," he said ominously. "It was a threat."

"What kind of threat?"

"Against Vannie. He said 'Vanessa will die!'"

I'd already tucked the earlier threat and the brick into my hip pack thinking I'd probably made too much of it, that Trina could be right. Now the hope of coincidence washed out of me and fear surged in. Meredith's death alone was horrible. Unthinkable. A solemn but harmless woman, she'd fallen victim to a killer who had a personal grudge about which we knew nothing. Now it seemed the entire Bradley family had been targeted.

"Why?" I said aloud, but to myself.

"I can't imagine," Marty answered. "She's a fine young woman. Meredith was so proud of her."

"How much do you know about Vanessa?" I asked him. "Maybe there's someone from her other life who wants to hurt her." I meant, of course, her life with the adoptive parents, not her life as Joan of Arc that Trina had suggested.

"I don't know much at all, but I'm sure there wasn't any trouble there. Vannie would've told us. She's very straightforward."

"What about her father, Marty? Did Meredith talk to you about this?" If ever there was a wrong time to ask about the men who'd preceded him, surely this was it. Unfortunately for us all, murder wipes away the rules of propriety and forces the foul-smelling detritus of our lives to the surface like a lake turning over in spring.

"Vannie's father? Sure, Mere told me as much as I needed to know about that before we were ever married." He reached absently for the cigarettes that weren't in his pocket. Giving up a bad habit can be inconvenient at times like that.

"I'm sorry I have to drag you through this, Marty. I'd give anything if . . . but it's my job to dig into the past if it could have something to do with Meredith's death."

Sundance nudged my arm, in sympathy or eagerness to get moving. I scratched his face, feeling the need to provide comfort to someone.

"I'd glad you're asking. The kids, along with everyone else in town, tiptoe around, whispering and biting off words. When I try to talk about Mere, they hush me up, like not saying it means not thinking about her. Even the preacher couldn't let me talk tonight. He kept circling around the real words."

Oh please, I prayed. Get me out of this.

"Go ahead and talk, Marty," I told him, because what else could I do?

"She was always an honest woman. You asked if I knew about Vannie before. As soon as Mere and I started to get serious about each other, she took me into the kitchen at her mother's house. It was springtime and still coolish at night, but she opened the back door anyway. Later on I saw she was making it easy for me to run out if I wanted to."

He stuck his hands in his pockets and shivered as if still feeling the chilly breeze from that night. I thought I felt it, too.

"She told me she'd had a child. The whole story. About the boy, who'd gone to Vietnam right after their time together and never come back. And she said even if he'd lived and offered to marry her, she wouldn't have done anything different than what she did."

At least I knew something about Vanessa's father now. I wondered if Meredith had lied about not changing her mind if the boy had lived, or if she'd only said that to assure Marty that he wasn't her second choice.

"I can tell you, I was struck speechless. Not because of what she'd told me so much as that she had told me. By that time, of course, I was crazy over her and nothing could've talked me out of it. All the same, it took me a while to get fully used to the idea. By the time Vannie showed up here, I'd forgotten that Mere had told me. Blocked it out, I guess."

"I'm trying to imagine how a young girl works up the courage to tell her boyfriend that she's had a baby." And I wondered how I'd take the news if Wayne suddenly announced that he had a litter somewhere. Maybe I'd run a background check on him, just so there wouldn't be any unpleasant surprises later on.

"Mere had extraordinary strength. It takes that to say what you think. The rest of us don't really listen, you know? We hear what we want. I don't believe Mere ever told me anything but the truth. Never acted any way but what she meant. And for most of our life together, I guess I put meaning to her words that wasn't there at all. How can two people love each other without even listening and knowing?"

"Maybe," I said with cynicism, "that's how they do manage to stay in love. By not knowing the real person."

"Now, Kay." Marty took his hands out of his pockets and placed them firmly on my shoulders. "You ought to have a brighter outlook than that. You're young and in love and the future is still ahead of you."

All that was over for Marty, though, wasn't it? I felt my eyes beginning to sting and was glad the streetlight was behind me so that Marty couldn't see my face.

"But I'm keeping you from work and you've got your hands full, what with all our problems."

He had that right. "Look, Marty. I want all of you

to stick close together for the next few days," I told him. "You aren't planning to open the lumber store tomorrow, are you? Or the Tea Room?"

"No, not until it's all over." He meant the funeral, not the pain.

"Call the PD immediately if anything seems off-kilter. The least little thing."

His tanned face melted into the saddest smile I'd ever seen. "Thank you, Kay. You're being a good friend."

Ah, but would you say that, Marty, if you knew I'd been thinking of Vanessa as the only suspect in this case? I gave him a hug and sent him back inside with instructions to lock all the doors and windows.

I tugged on the lead rope and the quick-release knot untangled itself. Holding the reins and some mane in my left hand, I reached with my right to grab the saddle, but something was in my way. Ducking under Sun's neck, I found the note paper-clipped to the saddle. It was a flyer from Brother-hood of Strength, with a notation in bold black marker: GET BACK WHERE YOU BELONG.

The rest of the shift was so quiet, I found myself talking to Sundance and pausing for his responses. As usual, his comments on the current state of affairs were restricted to neigh-saying.

Feeling the need for more than sweet feedback, I rode down Morning Glory Way, hoping to find Delia at home. The lights were on in her living room and I took that as a good sign. Unless, of course, she and Roger had retreated to the bedroom in such a pas-sionate rush they'd forgotten to turn them off.

Across the street, yellow tape protected the Bradley house from the intrusion of ordinary life. While the other homes on the street were having their dishes dirtied and cleaned, their shades opened and closed, and their rooms filled with the breath of the living, that house remained frozen in time. Until the TBI released it and the Bradleys moved back in, the structure was a captive, just as the family would be until someone gave them the answers they needed to settle with death and go on.

I tied Sundance to Delia's tree and stomped up onto her porch, hoping the sound would alert those inside that company was coming—in case they needed to rearrange themselves first. My consideration was wasted, I gathered, since Delia opened the door before I had a chance to knock.

"Kay!" she said. "I thought you were the lynch mob."

"Lynch mob? Have you been practicing pagan rituals on the town square again?"

Delia had caused quite a stir a few years back when she'd started doing yoga exercises down at the memorial park. Eventually she'd given that up, not because a few prudish neighbors were offended, but because Delia had embarrassed herself by attempting positions so advanced she often had to be helped out of them.

"It's Roger I'm worried about," she said. "Come on in. We may need official intervention. He decided to attend the UFO meeting."

I could understand Delia's concern. UFO—Universal Friends Organization—was the club started by Mayor Mooten to study extraterrestrials in hopes of learning how to convince them not to zap our planet and eat our species. Assuming that was their intention. Mayor Mooten himself wasn't sure why such advanced beings hadn't already taken over the planet.

"Has Roger made contact with the aliens?" I asked.

I shoved a stack of magazines aside and took their place on the couch. Delia, who doesn't spend a third of her time in the saddle, perched on the brick hearth.

"No telling what claims he'll make, but we can safely bet the farm he'll stir up the crowd. He heard about last night's UFO sighting and felt he ought to become more involved. Now that he realizes the potential for fun."

"Poor Roger," I said. "Didn't anybody tell him that no one found the spaceship?"

"Oh, he's aware of that. He feels the search wasn't as thorough as it might have been."

"I think Roger's right. The aliens are among us." I offered her the flyer I'd found attached to Sun's saddle and watched her eyebrows shoot up.

"My dear, you're wrong," she said at last. "The aliens are an advanced species. This Brotherhood of Strength can't claim that."

"At least all the words are spelled correctly."

"Even more frightening," she said. "This reminds me of that letter to the editor the Benton Harbor paper ran a couple of years ago. Someone objected to an animal rights groups' concern about the spotted owl. I quote. 'Everybody knows those animal rights activists are just a bunch of vegetarians!' "

I could see how that would have annoyed Delia. She hasn't yet gotten over God's rejection of Cain's agricultural offering. The Brotherhood of Strength had stepped on another of her firm convictions— that women have rights.

"Have you heard of this group?" I took the flyer from her hand, refolded it, and tucked it into my pocket.

"Not until now. You can be sure I'll watch out for them from now on, though."

Just what Delia needed, I thought. Another cause. "Can you think of anyone who's likely to be a member?"

She thought for a moment, then said, "Anyone who seems more than a little taken with Henry's Simpler Times policy. Someone who wants to return to the days when all problems were solved by blaming a group he's afraid of."

"We don't have to go back in time for that," I pointed out. "I can't see how Henry's plan to return to the good old days tallies with his conviction that aliens are among us."

"I imagine the aliens are his scapegoat. Fear them, and the differences they bring. Avoid new ideas. Stay away from foreign influences. Everything you need is right here in Jesus Creek."

"Sad to think anybody could fill all their needs right here, isn't it?"

Delia sighed. "And then you wonder about people like Bruce Bradley. He was free, and he came back. To start a business? What was the boy thinking?"

"Well, he's the only child. I guess he felt he had to be here for his parents."

"You're forgetting Vanessa. And it's not as if Marty and Meredith were feeble. Bruce couldn't have known Marty would be alone so soon. You know what I think?" She leaned forward in a conspirator's pose. "I'll bet Meredith ordered him back here."

I couldn't imagine why she'd do such a thing, and said so. "Meredith would have encouraged him to go somewhere he'd have a better chance at success. Especially to open a business like the Tea Room, Jesus Creek would be a poor choice."

"But Meredith was opposed to the Tea Room," Delia reminded me. "And you have to wonder how she defined success. Why didn't she ever enlarge the flower shop? Why didn't she hire extra help and offer full delivery? I think Meredith was afraid to take risks and was determined not to let her son take any, either."

I'd never heard anyone say such things about Meredith Bradley, and my first inclination was to defend her against Delia's charges. Before I could form a rebuttal, however, I remembered why I so often go to Delia when I'm confused—she sees more than most.

Earlier, when I'd mentioned her pagan rituals, I'd been only half kidding. In another time, Delia would have been the village witch; townsfolk would have sought her out for herbal cures, love potions, and predictions about crops and weather. It wasn't that I believed she had extraordinary powers, but Delia's perception was keener than most anybody's. She studied people and thought about their words and actions, and about the discrepancies between the two.

More than that, she had lived across the street from the Bradleys for a long time and probably knew a lot about them that she'd never told. Delia is discreet with her knowledge.

"You sound as if you didn't like Meredith," I said.

"I didn't dislike her. Meredith Bradley never invited anyone into her life. She accepted customers as means to her end. I'm sure she was fond of her family, but I've always felt she loved them because it was her responsibility to do so."

"Surely not! I mean, she must have loved her kids. She's their mother."

Delia gave me an indulgent smile. "You overestimate us," she said. "Giving birth is a physical process. Has nothing to do with emotion."

"But what about all these women who—"

"And what about the women who torture and murder their own babies, sometimes in the name of love? I don't doubt Meredith did exactly what she thought was best for Bruce and Vanessa. That doesn't mean it was the best thing for them."

Delia had certainly tweaked at my own fears. If I ever felt the urge to have a family of my own, I'd remember what we'd just talked about. With that in mind, it would take more courage than I possessed to attempt motherhood.

CHAPTER

7

THE BURDEN OF RESPONSIBILITY WEIGHED heavily upon German Hunt. When I arrived at the PD on Monday afternoon, the acting chief was halfway down Al's throat and headed for his liver. Normally I let the boys work out their problems on their own, but when German turned a complaint about illegible log entries into a personal attack on Al's parentage, I felt I had to step in.

"Hey!" I shouted, to make myself heard over the accusations and denials. "Go to your corners."

"You stay out of this!" German turned on me and stuck a finger in my face. "Just shut the hell up!"

"You have three seconds to get out of my face," I told him through gritted teeth. "After that I'll bite off that finger and feed it to your dog." I didn't have to be loud anymore. My voice had dropped down to a level German recognized from some of our previous arguments.

He isn't the brightest man who ever walked, but German knows I don't make idle threats. He learned that after I offered to take a whip to him if I ever again saw him using one on a horse. I won't go into detail, but you may rest assured that German's horse will never receive another spanking. Al has never known the force of my wrath—he was just happy to be rescued. Both of them backed down an inch and stood shuffling their feet and hanging their heads like little boys caught with chocolate icing on their faces.

"Now just what is going on here?" I waited with arms folded across my chest. "Well?"

German erupted in explanation. "He made such a mess of the log I couldn't even read it!"

"Put your glasses on!" Al retorted.

"One at a time," I said. "And let's behave like little gentlemen."

For fifteen minutes I sorted through accusations, explanations, and excuses, while German and Al pouted. In the end I discovered there was no story. German hadn't been able to make out a word in the morning's log. Instead of asking Al to decipher it, German had pitched a tantrum. Instead of drinking coffee until German ran out of steam, Al had responded with a comment about illiteracy. Thus do all great wars begin.

They were still hissing at each other when I took the beeper and sent German out the door for the day. Turning back to Al, I asked, "Except for that, did anything interesting happen since I went home last night?"

"Yeah," he said eagerly. Knowing he was in disgrace, Al wanted to win back my favor with efficient and cheerful assistance. "Miz Jackson called about noon. Thank goodness she didn't come back here with those brats!"

"Hasn't Jen picked up the kids by now?"

Al shook his head. "She's still missing. What'll you bet she took off with somebody who can keep her in better style than Billy can?"

"Do you know Billy and Jen well?"

"I don't have to know him well to know somebody dropped a wrench on his head when he was a baby." Al grinned, amused by his explanation for Billy Atwater's shortcomings.

Billy had been a few grades ahead of me in school but I'd been aware of him. Every girl was. Billy Atwater had been—and still was, come to think of it—a hunk. I'd lusted after him just the way my girlfriends had, but Billy reserved his attention for two things—beat-up old cars and Jennifer Jackson. You never saw him without at least one of the two.

After graduation he'd taken a job at Proctor's Gas Station and was soon promoted to mechanic, leaving Mr. Proctor free to run the pumps. And shortly before Jen graduated, somewhere around the middle of our scholastically lackluster class, she'd become pregnant and they'd married. They lived quietly and happily, so far as I know, in an unremarkable rental house on the west side of town.

Now and then I'd see them driving past with the car full of kids, and all seemed rosy. When Jen and I stopped to chat in the grocery store, we'd engage in pointless and repetitive conversation. Living with Billy really hadn't prepared her for philosophical discussions at the produce bin, I guess. She'd never registered a complaint within my range of hearing, and I doubted Billy had enough wattage to think about the level of satisfaction provided by marriage.

"I'll stop by and talk to Billy. Wonder if he's at

work, or waiting at home for Jen?" That was an image to bring tears to your eyes.

"You want me to call and find out?" Al's hand was already on the phone.

"Naw. I've got nothing else to do, except track down Jason, find out what this Brotherhood of Strength is up to, and apprehend Meredith Bradley's killer."

"Oh, that's all fixed up." Al grinned so proudly I thought he'd solved the case himself.

"The TBI arrested Vanessa Hyland. You know, Meredith's illegitimate daughter?"

"What?" I nearly dropped the beeper I'd been struggling to attach to my belt. "When did this happen?"

"About two or three o'clock this morning. That's what Bill said, but he was probably sound asleep at the time, so I don't know for sure."

I was halfway out the door before he finished casting aspersions on Bill's diligence. By now Marty or the others would have contacted a lawyer and the wheels would be grinding, but there was no telling what indiscreet comments Vanessa might have made in the wee hours.

The arrest didn't surprise me—not after Mark Warner's comments Saturday night—but I'd assumed Vanessa had slipped down lower on the suspect list after that brick incident.

I had some subpoenas to return to Dwight Devereux Maddox anyway, and this seemed like the ideal time to pay him a visit. I spun around, collected the papers, and headed out for good, this time walking briskly in the direction of the Maddox law office.

It did not escape my notice that I was both the first officer on the scene and a potential defense witness. One way or another, I was going to be called to testify. Ethically, I should have kept everything I knew to myself until I was forced onto the witness stand, but it seemed to me that if I handled the conversation carefully, I could learn enough to satisfy my curiosity and maybe even pick up a lead to follow.

I burst through the door of Maddox's office like a tornado, catching his assistant off guard. Jeanne Newton was leaning back in a comfy leather chair with her feet propped on the desk in front of her. She had a cigarette in one hand, a Dr Pepper in the other, and the telephone receiver propped against her shoulder. She waved the soft drink at me and continued talking.

"Well, I'll sure tell him about that . . . you bet . . . of course, I wouldn't know a thing about it, but I'll tell D.D. you called. Thanks now. Bye-bye."

She carefully replaced the receiver with her cigarette hand and smiled as if she had waited all her life to share breathing space with me. "You want a Coke?"

"Sure," I said. "What kind have you got?"

"Dr Pepper and Diet Pepsi, in the fridge there. Help yourself."

I dropped the subpoenas on top of one of the piles already cluttering her desk and helped myself to a soft drink. Then I took one of the chairs intended for clients and made myself comfortable, although I stopped short of propping my own feet on the desk. "I heard Vanessa Hyland was arrested last night," I said.

Jeanne and I could call ourselves friends, but this was the first time I'd been stuck between one of her clients and the law. The situation was not covered at the academy, where it had been implied that all defense lawyers were out to take my worldly goods, denigrate me personally, and skewer me professionally. You could say I found myself in an awkward situation.

"I was the first one there after Marty found the body," I began, careful not to tell her any more than she would already know from the record. "Then the TBI took over. I don't know what they have, but it may be a strong case and Vanessa could have done it."

"Of course she didn't do it," Jeanne corrected me.

I wasn't about to debate our class valedictorian so I let her opinion pass unchallenged. "Do you know that the Bradleys have received threats since the murder?"

"Uh-huh," Jeanne said coolly.

"A note tied to a brick was thrown through their window. I was there shortly after and I've got it locked up."

Jeanne crushed out her cigarette and took a swig of the soft drink. "Uh-huh," she said.

"And you know about the phone call, too? I was there when it came in. So was Vanessa. She couldn't possibly have made the call herself, and she was in church when the brick went through that window, so she couldn't have done that, either, which means someone has it in for the entire Bradley family, and that someone may have killed Meredith."

"Take a drink of that Pepsi and catch your breath," Jeanne advised. "Now, would you be willing to testify?"

"Well . . . sure. If I have to. But I was hoping it wouldn't come to that. To trial, I mean."

Jeanne is almost as knowledgeable about the law as the man she works for. Most of us just go to her with our questions, and that confidence in the woman was the reason I hadn't even asked to see D.D. She's every bit as cool as her boss, too, but I was sure I saw her lean forward with a hint of eagerness.

"Really?" she said. "And why were you hoping that? Of course, we could save everybody a lot of time and money if you'd just go ahead and arrest the guilty party."

"Look, Jeanne. This is very frustrating. And exhausting. I know you won't say anything to compromise this case, and I'm trying really hard not to betray my side. The trouble is, I'm not practiced at this. I don't hang around lawyers all day."

"Lucky you."

"I'm just going to say as much as I dare, and you have to promise not to use it against me. Okay?"

Jeanne finished off her drink and tossed the empty can into a recycling bin on the far side of the room. If she'd been on our basketball team, County High might've won a game.

Finally she said, "If you say something that might prove useful to us, I'll have to tell D.D. But I won't deliberately try to get you in hot water. That's the best I can do."

Couldn't ask for more than that, could I?

"Okay. For reasons that make no sense even to me, I'd love to find out that Vanessa didn't kill her mother. There's no evidence I'm aware of that can save her."

"To warrant a conviction solely on circumstantial evidence—which is all you've got—the rule in Tennessee is that the evidence must not only be consistent with the guilt of the accused, it must also be inconsistent with her innocence." Jeanne grinned impishly at her own use of legalese. "And since Vanessa is innocent, and you folks haven't really got much of a case, I'd say you're going to get your wish."

I'm sure she was making a sincere effort to be normal, but Jeanne had worked for a cutthroat lawyer for far too long to let down her defenses. Fortunately, I have never been able to keep my feet out of my mouth, so I've gotten used to saying all the wrong things and it seldom bothers me these days.

"Just give me a lead," I begged. "The TBI will have put together a solid case against Vanessa, and they probably aren't looking for alternatives. If there's one single piece of information that indicates another suspect, tell me. I'll track it as best I can. Our resources aren't much, but I'll try. Just give me a reason to believe Vanessa is innocent."

I guess no one had ever said anything like that to her before, because Jeanne was momentarily speechless. It was undoubtedly an event that would never be witnessed again.

"As soon as D.D. gets back, I'll pass on your message," she said at last.

"Does that mean you don't have the least bit of evidence suggesting someone else could've killed Meredith?" The lead weight in my stomach told me it meant exactly that.

I hadn't expected anything else, of course. Vanessa was guilty of murder and we all knew it.

"Well, I guess D.D. can find me if he wants." I stood up and looked around for a place to dispose of my half-finished drink.

"You can leave that on the desk," Jeanne said. "And thanks, Kay."

It didn't seem I'd done anything to earn her gratitude, but Jeanne's always been polite. She had a proper Southern upbringing, you see.

"Hey, Kay?"

I stopped with my hand on the door and looked back at her.

"What are your reasons? For wanting Vanessa to be innocent, I mean?"

Delia could have put it in sensible order, but I hadn't had the foresight to run it past her. I'd have to go it alone. "Trina told me the other day that she thinks Vanessa was Joan of Arc in a previous life. I don't know whether Trina really meant it, whether she actually believes in reincarnation. Heck, I don't know whether I believe it."

Jeanne listened intently as I babbled. I had a vision of myself on the witness stand, red-faced and flustered as D. D. Maddox asked if my investigation had included a background check on any French saints.

"I don't know Vanessa well. I can't even say that I like her, but I understand what Trina meant. There's something about Vanessa that makes you think she's—I don't know. Special? Different from the rest of us. It's like she comes from another world."

The part of my brain that functions was screaming at me to shut up. Next you'll be wondering if Vanessa arrived in a UFO, it said.

"Jeanne, don't you dare repeat what I just said," I warned.

"Hey, Officer Martin, did you forget to read yourself your rights?" She laughed and lit another cigarette.

The somewhat one-sided conversation with Jeanne left me feeling unsettled. If German or— heaven forbid!—Mark Warner found out I'd gone to Vanessa's defense attorney and all but offered to work for the enemy, I'd be sporting the latest in tar-and-feather fashion.

Not that the TBI had anything to worry about. The case against Vanessa seemed solid to me. The only people who believed in her innocence were the Bradleys, and even they might be less inclined to defend her now that she'd been arrested.

Was Vanessa a kamikaze? I wondered. Had she come to this foreign town full of strangers knowing she'd commit a crime, be arrested, and face the consequences alone?

Why? I needed to know that, and since the TBI had sewn up the investigation of who, I was free to delve into the more interesting riddle of motive.

I walked back to the PD and pushed Al away from his desk. "I have to make some phone calls," I told him. "Go out and grab a sandwich while you have the chance."

He didn't need telling twice. As soon as my eager dispatcher was out the door, I picked up the phone and started dialing. First I had to get some basic information from the Bradleys, and I was glad Trina answered.

"Well, sure we've called Vannie's parents," she said, astonished that I could think they'd over-looked that.

I was more than a little happy to hear this, since otherwise I'd have to go to them. In spite of Meredith's assurance that Vanessa had been adopted and raised by a fine, loving couple, I would not be convinced of it until I'd met and judged the Hylands myself. If they turned out to be brutally abusive, then maybe I'd understand why Vanessa had felt such hatred for Meredith that she'd killed her.

"Listen, Trina. I'd like to talk to them right away. When do you expect them in?"

"Oh, no. You see, Mr. and Mrs. Hyland are away from home. They're in a travel trailer somewhere in Alaska. What I meant was, we've called their house. The house sitter will pass on the message as soon as they check in." Trina sounded breathless. She'd probably been running all morning, coping with this new disaster.

"When does the house sitter expect to hear from them? And why are they calling there? Shouldn't they talk to Vanessa while they're in the wilds of Alaska?"

There was a teeth-grinding pause before she explained. "Ordinarily they call Vannie every week, but there's no one to answer the phone now that Marty's been kicked out of his house."

Even though I'd had nothing to do with sealing off that house, and couldn't have given the family access to it if I had been in charge, it was clear that Trina's acid comment was directed at me.

"I see," I said tonelessly. "Please have the Hylands contact me as quickly as possible."

"I'll tell them," Trina promised. "I have to go now."

She didn't exactly slam the receiver in my ear, but close enough. Probably not the day to ask for that astrological chart, I thought.

Next on my list was the Department of Records and Archives. My call had to be transferred three times before someone useful picked up.

"What county?" the no-nonsense Ms. Jones asked.

"Jesus Creek is the county seat of Angela County," I said, surprised she didn't know that.

"The birth was recorded in Angela?" she confirmed.

"No. I don't know. I have no idea where she was born, but I hope it was in Tennessee. Can't you just check using the mother's maiden name?" I'd done well to remember to get that much information from the TBI's report in the office. In fact, I'd been quite proud of myself for thinking to look it up.

Ms. Jones was not so impressed. "That could take quite a while," she warned. "Why don't you call back when you have more information?"

It was not her words but her tone that set me off. I had visions of myself traipsing all over town, looking for every identifying number that had ever been attached to Meredith and then having to fill out a dozen official request forms in triplicate.

"Miss Jones," I said firmly. "I need that birth certificate in connection with a murder investigation and I need it yesterday. Now please use the information I've given you and let me know the instant you have something."

Ms. Jones must have dealt with a lot of pushy cops in her time because I hadn't intimidated her at all. "I'll do what I can," she said coolly. "Don't expect miracles."

Al had the misfortune to return just as the call ended. I shoved Ms. Faye Jones's phone number at him. "You see this? I want you to call her every half hour until she has that birth certificate, and I want her to read every word of it to you."

"Can I just have her fax it?" he asked eagerly.

Even though we've had the computer for a while, Al had only recently deciphered the formula for making faxed messages come and go. He was delighted with his new toy and went out of his way to find excuses to use it. This time he had a legitimate reason.

"That will be fine, Al," I said. "But before she can fax it, she'll have to find it. Remember—every half hour until she comes through."

He looked at his watch and started counting.

I decided to leave Sundance in the pasture until I was ready to patrol, rather than tying him to another tree. Odds were good I'd be thrown out on my tail anyway and would be on patrol within the half hour. Why shouldn't the Bradleys hold me responsible? I blamed me for Vanessa's arrest even though there was nothing I could have done to prevent it.

Oh, I might have launched my own investigation, but lacking equipment and personnel, could the Jesus Creek PD have found the vital clue that would lead to the real killer? I hadn't found anything to suggest that a single, solitary soul had gone near Meredith at the time of her death. Either she'd committed suicide, arranged her body on the floor eight feet away, then trashed her shop—or Vanessa had killed her mother.

Unlike television, real life is dreadfully mundane. The likeliest suspect is usually the guilty party. Realistically, I knew, the TBI had probably arrested the real killer. They don't like being embarrassed in court, either—nor are they lazy. If there'd been any other suspect, Mark Warner and his team would have followed up on it.

If Vanessa hadn't killed her mother, then some clever mind had devised and executed the perfect crime, and we mere mortals were unlikely to expose the twisted truth.

I had to threaten my feet to get them to make the journey down the highway, and the walk took twice as long as it should have. It seemed like days later when I arrived at Bruce and Trina's near-cottage and stepped reluctantly up to their door.

My timid knock brought a red-eyed Trina to the door. "Kay!" she said. Then she did something I never would have expected—she threw her arms around me and hugged me till it hurt.

Food was everywhere, and sympathizers were packed into the little house, happily chatting and gorging themselves. Two gray-haired ladies in church suits were washing and drying dishes to keep the soup line moving.

"Kay, I'm so sorry for being short with you earlier. We've had people coming and going all morning, the phone's been ringing off the wall, Marty's nerves are shot—"

"It's all right, Trina. I know you've got a lot on your mind, and I'm sorry to add to it. Is Bruce here? I really need to talk to him." Intruding on their grief was bad enough; I deserved to be flogged for pulling her husband away from her and leaving Trina to cope with Marty and the masses.

"He's in the kitchen. Come on. Have a plate while you're here." Trina took my arm and started to drag me into the heart of the mob.

"I need to talk to him privately," I said quickly. "In a back room, maybe?"

Her reluctance was plain, but Trina wasn't sure she could turn down my request without making the situation worse. Three people were seated in the living room, eating from dishes balanced on their knees. Every one of them watched and listened shamelessly, probably conjuring rumors of Bruce's imminent arrest. Neither of us wanted a scene, so Trina quietly directed me down the short hallway to their bedroom with a promise to send Bruce right along.

Like the rest of the house, the bedroom was small

and cramped. Lacking a closet, the young Bradleys used makeshift storage—a five drawer chest, a battered trunk, and plastic milk crates turned on edge and stacked against the wall. Trina's collection of pastel-colored scarves were hung from the windows, serving a dual purpose—fashion accessories and window curtains.

The king-sized bed filled all but a few inches of the remaining floor. Either there'd been no time to make it or Trina was as lax about such chores as I am. I, however, have never owned navy-blue satin sheets.

"Kay?" Bruce poked his head tentatively into the room. He appeared to be every bit as uncomfortable as I was.

"Sorry to interrupt," I said. It hadn't escaped my attention that the bed was the only place we could sit. Apparently Bruce and I had the same reservations about that, and we both wound up standing by the open door.

"Trina said you wanted to talk to me alone. That sounds ominous."

I assured him it wasn't, but the awkwardness of our setup—two adults crammed into a bedroom, both afraid to sit down and relax—made the meeting much more stressful than it should have been.

"First of all, I have no way to help Vanessa. I want you to know that I didn't learn about the arrest until it was a done deal."

"I know," Bruce said sweetly. "The TBI charged in and took control. If you'd been in charge—"

"The same thing would have happened. Just at a more reasonable hour. But here's the thing—the

TBI arrested the most likely suspect, and now they'll devote their time to strengthening their case. I'm willing to listen to all sides." That implied I was going to continue looking for other suspects, which wasn't the case at all. I don't have time to waste on pointless endeavors. On the other hand, I didn't expect Bruce to open up to me if I told him I was on a mission to find out why Vanessa had committed murder.

"You know we'll do whatever it takes," Bruce said. "This is crazy. Vannie didn't kill Mom."

"Tell me why you believe that, Bruce. Tell me about Vanessa." I wanted to sit with him in a quiet, peaceful place where the noise of cups clinking wouldn't intrude. "How did you feel when she popped up at the door claiming to be your sister?"

He smiled at my description of the belated blessed event. "It wasn't quite as dramatic as that. First Vannie sent a letter. That was several weeks before we met her. She wanted to give Mom the option of ignoring it."

"Thoughtful," I said. "But Meredith answered it."

"Of course! Dad and I wrote short notes, too, just so Vannie would know we were all happy to hear from her."

"Were you? Happy?"

He seemed almost embarrassed to admit it. "You know all that stuff you hear about sibling rivalry? When I was a kid, I always asked Santa Claus for a baby brother or sister. Every year! I made a list of the games we'd play. I even kept some of my toys in a special box and never played with them because I wanted to keep them new for when Santa came through."

"I'll bet you were on a St. Nick Blacklist," I said. "Didn't you ever mention this to your parents? You might've had more luck."

Bruce nodded. "When I was eight, I wrote a letter to Santa, asking for the same thing. Stuck it in the mailbox on my way to school. Sometimes the post office just doesn't get it, you know? They returned my letter because I'd forgotten to put a stamp on it. Mom opened it and saw what I'd ordered—by this time I'd started asking for a six-year-old brother or sister. Anyway, when I got home from school that day, Mom explained both Santa and babies. She told me that babies are expensive and that she and Dad couldn't afford another one."

"All your dreams crushed in one afternoon." I could have cried for the little boy he'd been.

"Just goes to show, you shouldn't give up on your dreams. Sometimes they come true."

"But Vanessa isn't a little sister. She's older than you by several years," I reminded him.

"Picky, picky. All in all, Vannie's about the best sister I could hope for. She's house-trained, she's never started a food fight, and she doesn't break my toys." Bruce couldn't have been prouder of a new puppy.

"Of course, you don't have to live with her," I said. "If the two of you had grown up under the same roof—"

"But we didn't. We're siblings in the only way we can be, Kay. I've loved getting to know Vannie, and I resent losing this time with her, especially now.

She's lost her mother, too, you know. Vannie
deserves to be here with us. We need her."

He was blaming me or begging, but I couldn't
decide which. It was as if Bruce grieved the loss of
his sister as much as the loss of his mother.

"I'd help if I could," I swore. I just didn't go so far
as to explain that I lacked his faith in Vanessa's
innocence.

"Kay, if you knew her better—"

"I wish I did. That's why I'm here, Bruce. Tell me
about Vanessa. Help me get to know her."

He did. For twenty minutes he went on about his
sister's patience, tolerance, wisdom, talent, and
charm. It seemed to me that Bruce and his family
were converts to the cult of the goddess Vanessa. He
praised her without reservation and never noticed
how I grew more and more impatient. By the time
he ran out of steam, I'd decided that the Bradleys
were under an evil spell.

"Come talk to Dad," Bruce insisted. "Ask him
about Vannie. He can even tell you stories about
Mom and Vannie together. That'll make him feel
good, too. He complains that we don't talk about
Mom enough."

The last thing on earth I wanted was to listen to
another tribute to Vanessa Hyland. The thought of
it made my stomach clutch, but I felt an obligation
to that family. If spending a few minutes with
Marty could ease his pain, how could I refuse? I followed Bruce down the hall to the kitchen, all the
while praying for my beeper to rescue me. I
wouldn't even have minded a Jason sighting.

* * *

"There's been a crowd here all day," Marty said.

At that moment a half-dozen people were milling through the house, enjoying the Protestants' pale version of a wake. Marty poured a cup of coffee for me from the just-brewed pot and offered a selection of pies, cakes, and cookies from the groaning countertop. "Everyone comes and eats but the food keeps increasing."

"We should send a doggie bag home with them all," Trina suggested.

"Or hand it out at the door like Halloween candy," Bruce said. "They're ghouls, pushing their way in here to see the family."

Marty and Trina looked at him with shock and disapproval. Trina reached out to cover Bruce's trembling hand with her own and rested her head against his arm.

"You're upset, son, but that's no excuse. Now it may be that some folks are curious, but you got to expect that. It doesn't mean they aren't genuinely sympathetic."

"Come on, Dad. If they aren't here to look for bloodstains, they're hoping we'll publicly accuse Vanessa!" Bruce's nerves were stretched to the snapping point, but his family didn't see it.

"Bruce, you're not being fair," Trina said quietly. She glanced nervously around to see if anyone else had heard him.

Before his family could try again to correct Bruce's attitude, I broke in. The tension in the room was already so thick I figured my questions couldn't make it any worse. "I just found out about Vanessa being arrested when I came on duty today. The TBI handled the case. The investigation was theirs, and with good reason—they've got equipment, manpower, and experts in every field. My point is, I have no idea what they've got. I don't know how much trouble Vanessa's in. I can read their reports, but Mr. Maddox will have done that already." I felt it was vital to make Marty understand that I'd had nothing to do with this particular pain he suffered.

All three of them looked at me with forgiving eyes, as if they were determined to excuse my error. Those hearts must have been big enough to shelter all the remorseful sinners in the state.

I went on. "Vanessa was the only one in the house when Meredith died. She benefits from Meredith's will. She had means, motive, and opportunity."

"So did I!" Bruce reminded me.

"But you have a sterling alibi. As do Trina and Marty."

"Yes, but someone threatened Vannie!" Marty protested. "You were there when the call came in. And you saw that note!"

"I've talked to Jeanne down at D. D. Maddox's office and told her that. If need be, I'll testify. But Marty, Vanessa is charged with murder, not vandalism."

"She could barely raise her head! She'd taken the Demerol for her headache!" Marty's face turned red and his cheeks puffed out like balloons.

The others in the house had ceased their chatter, the better to eavesdrop. Trina made a discreet shushing sound, reminding us to keep our voices down.

"Can we prove that? Vanessa said she took it, but there's no way to know exactly what condition she was in. The prosecutor will say she set up the perfect chance to commit the crime—home alone, with more than enough time to arrange the crime scene to her satisfaction, dispose of any incriminating evidence, and wash off traces of blood."

Marty was beaten. He mulled over the things I'd said, made a few false starts at rebuttal, then slumped in his chair and ran his hand across his face. Bruce and Trina were shrinking in their seats as well. If I'd gone there deliberately to crush the Bradley family, I couldn't have done a better job.

Proctor's Gas Station closes at five P.M. every day. That's when Mr. Proctor leaves, anyway. It's not unusual for Billy Atwater to hang around for several hours after that, tinkering with whatever's on the rack. As long as he's there, Billy will pump a tank of gas, wash a windshield, check the air and water, or just make change for the more self-sufficient customer.

It wasn't quite five when I got there, but Mr. Proctor had already left—one of the perks of semi-retirement, I guessed. Billy, as usual, was under the hood of a car and I had to walk right up and tap him on the shoulder before he noticed me.

"Oh, hi, Kay," he said, as if he'd expected to see me there.

His dull eyes could have been due to any one of many causes: a long and tiring day, worry about his wife's disappearance, intense concentration on the task at hand, or dwindling candlepower. I generously chose not to speculate further.

"Hey, Billy," I said. "Any word from Jen?"

"Not a one." He pulled an oil-soaked rag from his back pocket and used it to wipe his hands like he thought it would do some good. "I can't imagine where she'd have gone."

"Why didn't you tell us she'd gone missing?" I asked. "I heard about it from her mom."

"Yeah, she told me she'd gone to the police. I went over after work last night to get the kids, and Maedyne came tearing out of the house like the devil was after her. She said something about an APB on Jen?"

I stifled a laugh. It was not, after all, a matter to be taken lightly. "It hasn't come to that," I assured him. "We've all been keeping an eye out for Jen. On the other hand, Billy . . . if she doesn't turn up soon, it would be a good idea to increase the effort. Maybe even call in the FBI."

Billy's mouth dropped halfway to his chin. "You don't think something's happened to Jen, do you? Like her being kidnapped?"

"I just don't know," I said truthfully. "Has anyone asked you for ransom money?"

Billy thought for a minute, then decided he had received no such request. I was tempted to ask exactly when he'd noticed his wife was gone and who'd helped him to discover the discrepancy. "Aren't you the least bit worried about her?" I prodded.

"Well, I hadn' been, but now that you've brought up kidnapping . . ."

I thought if I could upset one more person, I'd have met my goal for the day. "Well, Billy," I said, exasperated, "what did you think had happened to her?"

He mopped his brow with the oily rag. He didn't appear nervous, only stressed by the effort of thought. "You know we've got three kids now."

Oh, yes. I remembered them well.

"I've been hearing on TV about how women like Jen need time off from the kids and the housework. I figured she'd just had a real rough week and decided to go off by herself for a while. You know, like a vacation?"

Frankly, I was surprised he'd have been aware of the stress in Jen's life. And they say television is destroying our minds. "As I understand it, Billy, she'd gone to the store for milk and she didn't come back. If Jen had planned to take a few days off, don't you think she'd have mentioned it? Packed a bag?"

After he'd chewed on that awhile, Billy threw the rag to the ground, squared his well-muscled shoulders and looked me right in the eye. "If anybody's hurt Jen," he said, "I reckon I'll have to kill him."

He said this as a statement of fact, and I believed he would follow through. In the interest of crime prevention, I tried to distract him by asking a few more questions.

Before I left, Billy had given me a list of names, everyone he could think of who might have heard from Jen. The whole of it had begun to sink into his tiny brain and Billy was practically trembling when I told him bye.

His mother-in-law had implied that Billy was somehow to blame for whatever had happened to Jen. Once he realized there might be a problem, he'd been genuinely concerned. I didn't believe he was smart enough to fake that or to do away with his wife without leaving a trail of incriminating evidence a mile wide.

I hoped, of course, that Billy had left out some small detail—a spat that had sent Jen off in a huff. Perhaps she was even then pouring out her heart to one of her friends. Otherwise Jen was in trouble somewhere and I hadn't taken it seriously until just that moment.

CHAPTER

8

BY THE TIME I ESCAPED FROM THE FUNERAL feast, I was stuffed full of casserole and cake. It's my theory that fat-laden food serves as a tranquilizer and that's why it is served and scarfed down during times of trouble or excitement.

What had I learned? I pondered the question as I trudged back to the PD. There was no doubt in my mind that the Bradleys sincerely believed in Vanessa's innocence. I had fleetingly considered the possibility that there was a family plot to destroy her with a show of loving support, but had to give it up when I couldn't explain it even to myself.

If I wanted to discover Vanessa's motive, I'd have to go to more objective sources. It didn't seem reasonable that she'd harbored a grudge against her mother for twenty-plus years, plotting and planning revenge without concocting an escape for herself. If it wasn't hate that had driven Vanessa to matricide, then what had?

There are only a handful of motives strong enough to give rise to murder. If I ruled out hatred and love, I could focus on the others. Anger? A sudden burst of fury that drove Vanessa to commit an unthinkable act for which she'd be forever sorry. Or greed? Perhaps Meredith had been duped into leaving all her worldly goods to her elder child.

I've found, though, that the most common cause of misery is a desire for power. We all want it, need it, go lusting after it with reckless determination. I've seen the need for it turn meek, socially challenged toads into brutally abusive husbands and fathers. The sweet little women who have lived for decades without raising their voices heed the call of Power when given the presidency of the garden club. Some of us find our domination in controlling a huge beast, or in carrying a gun.

Placing my bet on this as a motive, I tried to figure out how Vanessa perceived murder. Two semesters of general psychology had not given me enough to work with. Unless it was the power over life and death that Vanessa craved, I was at a loss. Temporarily. Lucky for me, I'd befriended an excellent psychologist in Nashville to whom I could turn for answers.

Al met me at the door, flapping a piece of paper in my face. "I got it!" he shouted. "Only took me three phone calls. You just gotta get tough with these state employees."

I snatched the fax from his hand and skimmed through it, praying there'd be no blank spaces. Indeed, Vanessa had been born to Meredith on April 15, 1967, in Robertson County, Tennessee. The father's name was given as James McCrary, but there was no further useful information. My next step would be to check military records, to see if Meredith had told her husband the whole truth.

And then I had a better idea. "Al," I said, "you've done a great job! I couldn't get anywhere with that woman at state records."

"Well," he drawled modestly, "you just gotta take the right attitude with 'em."

"I tried my best, but if not for you, I'd still be haggling. You are truly a miracle worker." I gave him an appreciative pat on the arm.

"Just glad I could help out," Al said humbly. "Any time you need my help—"

"Really? You mean that? Because I'm really dreading this next one. See, I've got to find some military records."

And *that*, friends, is a prime example of my devious use of power.

It was so late into the shift before I got to him that Sundance had decided I wasn't coming at all, and he liked the idea. Small as the pasture was, he managed to elude me for almost twenty minutes before he felt that he'd made his point. There is no way to catch a horse who doesn't want to be caught—not without a sure-shot lariat, anyway. I was determined to earn Sun's respect and cooperation, but I finally surrendered and bribed him over with a carrot. Respect would have to come another day.

By the time we started out to patrol the mean streets of small-town America, I was covered in sweat and grass stains, and my shoes carried an extra pound of horse poop. Fortunately, I don't begrudge Sun his little moments of rebellion. Who among us wants to be at another's beck and call?

Ambling down Main Street, I tried to forget the

frustrations that had already piled up on my shift and focus on the joy of the moment. The world looks different from the back of a horse. Leaves are individual works of art instead of the green blur that zips past at normal highway speed. Tiny wildflowers fairly jump out and demand to be noticed. People are more likely to wave and speak as you pass by, most of them terrifically envious (I like to think) of the rider.

On Monday evening Brother Wagoner and his neighbor, Gene Ballard, cut their lawn mower engines when Sun and I passed by. They both smiled and waited respectfully until they deemed it safe to make noise again. Sundance, of course, hadn't been the least bit worried about those growling mechanical monsters, but he accepted the tribute as any royal being would have.

The Veatches' yard was, as always, immaculate. Mr. Veatch is a bug about dethatching and mulching. His landscaping efforts lean toward the sophisticated except for a wild patch in the backyard where he's indulged the decadent inner man with an assortment of gaudy color and showy blooms. I have no idea how Mrs. Veatch feels about this, but from comments she's dropped here and there, I suspect she's happy with any yard that doesn't involve her participation in the digging, cutting, and weeding. Sensible woman.

I noticed in passing that someone—no doubt the softhearted lady of the house—had left a small, foil-covered cardboard box in plain view at the end of the driveway. It never occurred to me that the Veatches had put it there while collecting the mail and then forgotten to carry it inside. Around here it's not unusual to find packages like that, deliberately packed for the town's favorite charity case, Jason.

Sundance and I roamed the streets, chatting with folks who sat in swings or rockers on their front porches. We didn't learn much beyond the general health and attitude of the neighborhood, but sometimes that's enough. Meredith Bradley's death found its way into every conversation, as is to be expected. Everyone knew her, all were stunned by the murder, but few admitted to having been shocked by the news of Vanessa's arrest.

"We should've seen it coming," Mrs. Gray said. "Being deserted by her own mother and raised by strangers—why, it's no wonder that girl turned out like she did!"

Edith Gray wasn't blaming Meredith for bringing trouble on herself. Being a kind and compassionate soul, she was searching for a way to excuse Vanessa.

"I just don't know," she went on, "if Marty can make it on his own. He's tore up bad—had to run out of church the other night when the preacher was talking about the prodigal son. He didn't look much better after he got back, either. All the fresh air in the world can't pump up a broken heart. I expect he'll feel obligated to Meredith's girl now, being the kind of man he is."

"With all the new ones moving in here," Florence Healy opined, "it's a wonder we're not all murdered in our sleep!"

Miss Healy defines a newcomer as anyone who

hasn't been born of a fourth-generation Jesus Creekian. Since I am the fourth generation, she hasn't yet decided whether I'm one of them or not, and perhaps her remark was intended to remind me that I'm still on probation.

On down the street, Delia and Roger were cuddled up in her porch swing, watching the world go by. Roger held up a frosty mug of beer and shouted to me, "Ha ha! I've got a cold beverage and you haven't!"

I showed him my plastic bottle of tepid water. "Your old bones will freeze and crack while my youthful body remains warm and supple." I nudged Sundance across the overgrown lawn and up to Delia's porch.

"You're wise to take the evening shift," Delia said. "I saw German earlier today. It seems the noonday sun brings on swarms of insects. I see you're not bothered too much."

"They're still out," I assured her. "I just don't appeal to bugs the way he does."

I'd seen German and his horse fighting the flies that cling and bite all through the summer months. There's no way to be rid of them until winter, but through experimentation, I'd concocted a fly spray formula that worked a little better than the commercially packed stuff. I'd even offered to share my secret with German, but he rejected it just as he did Rhonda's instruction. Let him suffer.

"I saw a seven-layer salad at the Bradleys' that had sprouts on top," I said. "Guess you've been there."

"It's awkward, isn't it?" Delia sucked in her cheeks.

"Strange way to describe murder," Roger told her. "Awkward?"

"Usually someone dies, we take food to the house, we go to the funeral. This is alien territory, though. The house sealed up because it's a crime scene, the body off for autopsy. And now Meredith's daughter arrested! I'm sure Miss Manners would know exactly how to handle it, but damned if I do." Delia took a sip of her iced herb tea, her opinion of Vanessa left unspoken.

"You might try my method," Roger suggested. "Ignore it and pretend death will never strike you."

"That's clever," I said. "Pay it no mind and it'll go away." I closed my eyes and chanted, "Jason isn't there, Jason isn't there."

"You'll have to try harder than that," Roger warned. "I've been ignoring Henry Mooten for years, but his belief in his own existence is powerful. I just can't make him disappear."

"You haven't been ignoring Jen Atwater, have you?"

"I haven't even been aware of this person," Roger promised, "so how could I ignore her?"

That would have been a suspicious statement coming from anyone else in town, but Roger truly didn't know most people. That didn't stop him from offending them, though.

"Her mother was in the grocery store this morning," Delia said. "With a menagerie of wild beasts. I don't remember Jen being an unruly child."

"Scary, isn't it? Those kids have all that energy and probably Billy Atwater's brain. If Billy went missing, I'd just look in the closets to see which one he'd locked himself into."

"Jen's different though, isn't she?" Delia said.

"Yeah. Not the brightest student, but she's got common sense. Strange taste in men. I'm ready to believe there's more to this than a runaway wife. Surely she'd have contacted her mother, or a friend."

"I agree." Delia's mouth tightened as she contemplated the possibilities. "Jen and her mother always seemed close. She has a large group of acquaintances, and I've never heard anything to indicate that she and Billy don't get along."

"I really ought to keep an eye on him, though. Husbands surprise you. And he is the last person who'll admit to seeing Jen." I was thinking out loud, reminding myself of odds, and the odds said Billy was a prime suspect.

"Don't you hate it when your head tells you one thing and your stomach tells you another?" Delia gave me a sympathetic sigh, as if she'd been the tug-of-war rope too often herself.

"I wish I had the same problem with Vanessa Hyland," I confessed. "My head says she did it, and so does the rest of me. Marty and the others won't even consider the possibility, and they know her better than I do."

"They're too close," Delia said. "Which is odd in itself. How often do you find a family willing to accept a new member so readily? And under these circumstances, you'd expect Bruce to be particularly hostile toward Vanessa."

"Especially after he lost part of his inheritance to this long lost sister. Then again, Bruce is a sweet guy."

"Ah," Roger said, and held up one finger. "But that wife of his! Kind to animals, children, and spirits of the netherworld. It's unnatural to be so . . . pleasant. You don't suppose she's hiding a violent temper, hmmmm?"

"Now that you mention it, Roger, no animals were killed in the commission of the murder." I slapped my forehead. "I should have seen it before! Trina is clearly the guilty party!"

"You only had to ask for my assistance, dear." Roger finished off his drink, satisfied with his service to mankind.

"Relieved of that burden, I shall continue my patrol." I turned Sundance and prepared to leave the town's favorite couple to their evening pleasure, then remembered I hadn't gotten an update on Roger's club meeting.

"How was the UFO meeting, Rog?" I asked.

He placed his right hand solemnly above his heart. "My joy knows no boundary. I have been inducted!"

"And my surprise knows no boundary. You mean you weren't kicked out on your astros?" Henry Mooten and his friends clearly didn't demand a lot of their associates.

On the other hand, Henry may have been willing to overlook much of Roger's behavior because he felt indebted. It was Roger, after all, who gave Henry

the campaign slogan that helped get him elected—
For simple values and simpler times, vote for a
simple man.

"Was there an initiation ceremony?" I asked
eagerly. "Did you have to strip naked and paint
yourself blue?"

"And dance by the light of the moon," Roger sang.

"You danced and they still let you join?" Delia
asked with astonishment.

Roger tossed his head. "I was exquisite. They
were so blinded by my soft shoe, they didn't even
notice when I took control of their organization."

"Oh?" I wasn't sure this would be an improvement
over the excitable leadership the UFO group had
had before.

"Well, I've taken the first step toward total domination, anyway. I have been named vice-president
of UFO. It's only a matter of time before I replace
Henry as president, and once that happens—"

"You'll be the leader the aliens ask to be taken
to?" I offered.

"That, too. Meanwhile, I am chairing the committee for cataloguing alien sign."

He seemed quite proud of this, but I had no idea
why. "What does the committee do?" I foolishly
asked.

"Obviously they collect and catalogue alien sign,"
Roger explained. "Tracks, and whatever else the
aliens leave behind."

"You mean if aliens leave droppings in the woods,
you collect it?" I thought this must be the worst of
all possible committees and wondered why Roger
had allowed himself to be appointed.

"Not me personally, of course," he assured me. "My underlings search through the bushes and briars, collecting samples and so forth. Once it's photographed and bagged, they bring it to me."

"And what do you do with the alien poop, Roger?"

"What else?" he said, as if it should be obvious. "I identify the type of alien it came from."

Sundance and I made a dinner stop at the PD, where hay and water awaited. Normally I would have left Sun to roam free, depending on his fondness for food to keep him in place, but after the trouble I'd had catching him earlier, I decided he could not be trusted. I tied him to the hitching post and sat down on the sidewalk nearby to contemplate Life.

Actually, I contemplated Death. Meredith Bradley's. Vanessa had to be the killer and I ought to be dancing a jig because she was behind bars, not falling in with her family's loyal but baseless fantasies about her innocence. The Bradley family's feelings could not change the fact that Vanessa had means, opportunity, and motive. I knew the TBI had dug into her background, no doubt harassing everyone Vanessa had ever known. Had they found a dark tale in those records and interviews that might have served as a warning to Meredith? I wondered. And would Meredith have believed it if anyone had told her she was in danger? Or would her maternal instinct have denied even the possibility that her child meant to harm her?

I've learned not to dwell on the what-ifs. Aside from wasting precious time, that sort of speculation

can bury you under a pile of guilt so deep no thera-
pist will ever dig you out. What if I'd had oatmeal
instead of rice for breakfast and used less milk so
there'd be some left for the gravy tonight? Still, I
allowed myself the luxury of what if Meredith had
not opened her home to Vanessa?

It was hard dusk and in a few more minutes the
sun would drop below the river. I pulled Sundance
away from his feast, lifted myself into the saddle,
and made my way circuitously through alleys and
yards. A few people saw me but no one complained
or expressed surprise at finding a mounted police-
woman bumbling through the bushes. It takes a lot
more than that to stir up the hardy stock we've
grown here.

The widow Law was heading around the side of
her house, chasing after Purrsey, her clawless cat.
She called to me for help, not realizing a fire-
man was the traditional rescuer of wayward kitties.
Nevertheless, I rode over to provide moral support
as she pleaded with Purrsey to come out from under
the porch.

"Kitty, kitty," she crooned. "Mommy loves you.
Mommy won't hurt you."

I slid to the ground and, holding Sun's reins in
one hand, went to the opposite side of the wooden
porch. "I'll try to shoo him your way," I said.

The porch was backed against the house, and concrete steps closed off the fourth side, so Purrsey had
no choice if he wanted to run. I squatted by the
opening and made mildly threatening motions at
the cat. Purrsey was fascinated. I scowled and he
meowed.

"That's a good boy," Mrs. Law said encouragingly. Purrsey looked at her then sidled closer to me.

"Come here, sweetie." Mrs. Law was practically begging, but this did not influence her feline friend.

The cat's purring grew louder, more like a growl. My own cat does that just before she rips open the skin on my arms. I remembered Purrsey's inability to shred me, relaxed for a moment, then shot to my feet when the blinding light of realization struck. That was not Purrsey's purr, but the distant hum of a motorcycle's engine!

By the time I'd fumbled my way back into the saddle, Purrsey was racing across the yard with Mrs. Law in hot pursuit. I'd certainly owe her an apology, and I sincerely hoped she retrieved her pet before the neighborhood dogs did, but I had bigger catfish to fry.

Picking up on my adrenaline rush, Sundance wanted to take off, but I held him back in spite of myself. A motorcycle did not necessarily mean Jason's motorcycle. I didn't want to make a fool of myself by rushing into the street to head off an innocent biker, and I didn't want to frighten away Jason if it did turn out to be him.

Sun's ears and mine were alert as we listened to the approaching engine. I eased Sun into position at the corner of Mrs. Law's house, out of sight from the street but ready to take off at a second's notice. When it sounded as if the motorcycle couldn't get any closer, I let Sun take a few steps forward into the driveway.

Then the sound grew suddenly dim and I felt a swell of optimism. The engine was idling! I tore around the house to find the mysterious motor-cycle, complete with bareheaded rider, pulled up beside the cardboard box in the Veatches' driveway. Jason was astride the machine, but leaning to the left, his arm stretched to retrieve the offering left there for him.

Just as it had been in my frequent fantasies! I thought of reaching for my gun but the sheer size of a horse tends to draw attention. Before I could make up my mind about using heavy firepower, Jason glanced up. When he saw me grinning with delight, he spun his bike around and tore out of there like the hounds of Hell were nipping at his backside.

And we were. Against Rhonda's instructions, and to my great surprise, Sundance broke into a gallop that promised to overtake Jason's motorcycle within minutes. I worried that his hooves might slip on the pavement, but my greatest concern was that the spunky horse would decide to jump the bike when he reached it.

The joy of flying through the darkness on my trusty steed was equaled by the excitement of finally—finally!—catching up to Jason. I was gig-gling with delight and giddy with the sure knowl-edge that this time I could at least put a scare into the brat ahead of me.

We'd almost reached the end of Morning Glory and my mind registered a moment of concern about the sharp left turn coming up. As it happened, I didn't have to deal with that. Jason zoomed across the barrier curb and into the wooded area beyond.

Sundance must have decided he was following a

strange new breed of centaur, and he either liked it or was determined to stomp the upstart stallion because he followed Jason's bike right into the woods without a moment of hesitation.

For a full minute my euphoria continued and then I realized what I was doing. Rhonda's Rules of Riding specifically forbade galloping through the woods under the light of a crescent moon. This was even more dangerous for both horse and rider than galloping on pavement. An accident in the woods could leave us injured and lost for hours or days before we were found.

Never mind that, my wiser self said. Just hold on!

Jason was doing fine. He controlled the bike's movements and therefore knew ahead of time when he'd be swerving to avoid a tree. Sundance swerved without warning, then swerved again, tossing me back and forth and side to side like a sack of flour.

My elation evaporated. Terror replaced it and I soon found myself grabbing mane and screaming "Whoa!" in a voice at least two octaves above normal. Sundance ignored my pleas and traveled on into the night.

I saw the bike's headlight bouncing up and down, and then I felt Sun's takeoff as he jumped to clear the trench of a dry creek.

The greatest surprise was that I remained aboard, albeit not for long. During flight, I'd lost a stirrup, and immediately started sliding sideways, clinging desperately to Sun's sweaty neck. Looking up at his chin, I begged him to whoa, and I guess he felt that my position had destroyed his chance of running with the thoroughbreds. He stopped and eyed me with disgust as I untangled myself from the remaining stirrup and stood on solid ground.

Up ahead, Jason was still going. I could track him by the headlight that cut through the pitch-black woods. Sundance and I had spent so much time on those trails I could almost feel the bumps as he hit them.

Breathing hard, heart pounding, I stood there beside my exhausted horse and cursed myself aloud. After all those months of praying for a lucky break, I'd finally gotten it. Jason had been delivered into my hands and I'd lost him. I didn't deserve to catch Jason. In fact, it would serve me right if he lived the rest of his life free and untroubled by klutzes such as me.

I watched the headlight disappear behind thickening trees. There was no penance great enough, but at least I could walk back to town and give Sundance a break. If I hadn't paused to wipe the spiderwebs off my face, I'd have missed it. Jason's headlight suddenly illuminated the topmost branches of a very tall tree. For two seconds more the light danced madly, twirling in all directions, then disappeared into the ground.

For a time the only sounds in those woods were my own heavy breathing and the rumble of Sun's gut, and then I heard the bike's engine kick in. I smiled. At least, I consoled myself, Jason had not gotten away without bruises.

CHAPTER

9

TUESDAY MORNING WAS EVERY BIT AS HOT and muggy as the day before. I put on my regular riding clothes—stretch pants, T-shirt, socks, and hiking shoes—and topped off with a generous application of insect repellent. Then I packed a lunch and a plastic bottle full of ice and tucked those into my hip pack. If need be, I'd stay in the woods until my shift started at three P.M., and with the addition of my watch and first aid kit, I was prepared for a marathon search.

The diligent gardeners along Morning Glory Way were out and about, watering their hardy stock of blossoms or harvesting fresh veggies from mini-gardens in their yards. I turned down two offers of tomatoes and a desperate plea from Mrs. Hendricks to accept a bushel of zucchini. Why, I wondered, are so many people taken with the idea that their neighbors want leftovers? How come nobody ever offers me a quart of strawberries or the *first* mess of beans?

Mrs. Law was out mowing her yard in the relative cool of the morning. I was relieved to see Purrsey watching her through the window, although I must say he looked forlorn and resentful of his captive state.

German was on Pudding, clip-clopping along, trying his best to look like Marshal Dillon. I hailed him as an afterthought, realizing it would be wise to let someone know what I was up to and where I'd be.

"You don't have any way of knowing where he went after you fell off the horse," he said. "Why, he could've circled around and come back down here to camp in your backyard."

"I know that." I pushed humidity-limp hair off my forehead and wondered if German would ever understand my overwhelming need to catch Jason. "I'm sure I can find the spot where he went down, though. After that I'll follow the trail as far as it leads. It's worth a try."

"You could put all this energy into something worthwhile, you know."

"And what would that be?" I asked tartly. "We don't have any other open cases. There's precious little gang activity on Main Street these days. Face it, German. If not for Jason, this police department would be out of business. Are you suggesting we go that route?" I propped a hand on my hip and waited for his answer.

"Are you suggesting we'd be better off with a crime wave? Just what have you got against peace and quiet?" He sat up there on his horse, smirking at me.

"It's unnatural, German," I pointed out. "The entire population of this town appears to be highly ethical and law-abiding."

"Then how do you explain that funeral the Bradleys are gearing up for?" he asked.

It seemed a reasonable question, but of course, German had completely missed the point. "First of all, that's a major crime and the only one we've had in two years! And second, it was committed by an outsider. It's almost like the rest of us are incapable of breaking the law. Or too apathetic to do it. I'm telling you, German, that human nature demands rebellion against the rules. What's the matter with folks around here? Are they all mindless robots, shuffling through life without a thought of their own?"

German jerked on the reins to reprimand Pudding for her eagerness to move on, then gave me a glare that suggested he'd like to put a bit in my mouth. "Let me get this straight. You're upset because people do the right thing? Kay, you get stranger all the time."

"I know it sounds odd," I admitted. "But I'm telling you, there's something wrong when an entire police department has nothing better to do than halfheartedly chase after one petty thief. It seems to me there must be a whole lot simmering under the surface, and I'd rather know about it than be taken by surprise when it suddenly boils over."

"Well, if there is anything brewing, you just be sure it's your business before you stick your nose into it! For that matter, if you're so convinced the whole town is conspiring to overthrow the government, why aren't you snapping pictures through bedroom windows instead of chasing after Jason?"

"Because," I said with a flip of my head, "I intend

to set an example. I want it made clear that crime
will not be excused, no matter how cute or pitiful
folks find the perp. Let's nip future felonies in the
bud."

German just stared at me and said, "I think
you're obsessed."

"Am not," was my clever comeback.

"Fine, then. It's your time. Just be sure you're
back for shift change."

German's bad attitude went a long way toward
convincing me that I'd have to quit the force if he
ever got promoted to chief. I was half tempted to
make a sarcastic comment about Pam's tolerance,
then thought better of it. Could be his bad mood had
something to do with marital tension—they were
still in that adjustment stage, after all—and I definitely did not want to play Dear Abby.

"Don't worry about that. I've never missed a shift
yet."

German raised a stern eyebrow and moved out.
That was his way of having the last word even
though there was absolutely nothing to say in
response. Even German would have to admit my
work record is nearly perfect.

Our conversation had raised my blood pressure
and my body temperature. I regretted having said
anything to German about my concerns. Seriously,
though. Is it normal for an entire town to behave
so well?

Maybe Henry Mooten's vision of Utopia was
coming to life, or maybe he'd put something in the
drinking water to keep us in hand. I had no objection to the use of mind control to discourage crime;

I worried a lot, though, about the behavior of German and the other good guys. Why did they accept Jason's thefts so calmly, for instance? And why were the Bradleys diligently defending Vanessa, when they should have cursed her soul to eternal damnation?

I felt like a character in a science fiction movie. There were pods in the basement, but no one listened to my warning.

At the end of Morning Glory the trees rose up suddenly like a barrier, and for most people that's exactly what they were. All my life I'd been aware of the wooded acres, but even as a child I'd never thought of going past the oak sentries into that dark forest. When Rhonda suggested riding there, I'd been surprised, but Sundance and I had followed her in and fallen under a spell cast by woodland fairies. By the time I started chasing after Jason, the woods felt like home.

I started at just the spot where Jason and I had left the road the night before. The ground was hard and dusty, and it denied me all hope of tracking the motorcycle. Sun's hoofprints had made an impression clear enough to follow, but Sundance, of course, had stopped long before Jason did.

Undaunted, I tromped up the slight incline and followed the trail as it twisted and turned. Now and then I'd spot a fallen log or small clearing that I remembered passing the night before, and my optimism grew with those confirmations.

At one point I found the intersection of a wider trail suitable for four-wheeling, and wondered why Jason hadn't taken that relatively easy route.

Maybe he hadn't seen it in the dark, or hadn't been able to make the ninety-degree turn onto it. I preferred to think he'd been so surprised by my sudden appearance that he hadn't been thinking straight and so headed directly toward his lair. I liked the idea of Jason being terrified.

It took me almost forty-five minutes to find the signs of my unexpected dismount. I stood there and looked ahead, mentally erasing the shafts of sunlight that spurted through the tree canopy and replacing it with the shadow outlines that had been there the night before.

Moving slowly, I stayed on the trail, my eyes glued to the ground. When I finally reached the scene of Jason's undignified spill, I was gratified to see that he'd left the signs of a hard, scooting impact. I walked carefully around the edges, noting places where the bike's tires had skidded sideways, pushing aside leaves and sticks and gouging at the bare earth. The bike appeared to have hit a rut in the ground and gone flying toward the right. Judging by the scraped ground and cleared leaves, Jason had slid off toward the left.

Circling slowly, I hoped for a monumental stroke of luck. While finding a wallet with complete ID would have been nice, I could have settled happily for a scrap of paper, like a receipt for gasoline (assuming he bought it instead of stealing it) or even a scrap of fabric. Nothing like that smiled up at me.

"Whoa!" I said aloud, forgetting for a moment that my own two feet were the only ones moving. "What's that?"

At the outer edge of the skirmish area I squatted for a closer look. Sure enough, a miracle had occurred. In a patch of scraped dirt stood a pool of oil the size of my palm. When the bike went down, the crankcase must have been punctured.

The grin on my face would have frightened away a grizzly bear. If not the grin, the happy dance would have done the trick. I had my first lucky break, and I was ready to devote my life to following that oil trail. Tiny drops might hide in the foliage, but I would crawl on my hands and knees, searching the forest floor inch by mossy inch if that's what it took. At worst, the trail would end before I found Jason, but his bike would be out of commission until the crankcase was repaired. And at best, I'd be able to take in a prisoner before my shift even began.

The blast of a horn cut through my celebratory haze. It was so loud and clear I knew it had to be nearer than the street where I'd entered the woods, but how on earth would a car get into the woods? And it was a car horn—not the puny beeper found on a recreational vehicle or the basslike honk of an air horn.

I stopped analyzing that riddle to listen to the rhythm—three short blasts, three long, three short. I looked at the ground where Jason's trail waited and the emergency signal blared again.

Lucky Sundance wasn't there—he'd have been appalled by the words I used to express my displeasure. Still muttering vulgarities, I stomped through the woods toward the infuriating sound, crushing innocent wildflowers under my feet.

The horn kept honking until I caught myself stepping in time to the beat. When I reached the broad trail that intersected the one I was on, I waited, and sure enough, the call was coming from my left.

As I trudged off in that direction, I studied the trail. Hunters on their four-wheelers, Jason on a bike—yes, these could have made their way along the narrow path. A sturdy pickup, perhaps? One of the smaller size ones might have survived the trip, perhaps, but I didn't see any damage to the trees that held their branches so low I had to slap them away from my face.

I could tell from the volume that I was getting closer, and one more turn brought me into sight of a small clearing. In the clearing, beside a single maple sapling, sat a car. A 1974 Chevy. Tan, with the passenger side door primered gray.

From ten feet away I could see Jen Atwater inside, calmly sounding the alarm that had attracted me. My feet were in high speed motion before I even thought about running. Once I'd reached the clearing, I ripped open the car door with so much force it nearly came off in my hands.

"Jen! Are you okay?" I shouted.

She smiled serenely at me and said, "Why, Kay. How nice to see you. What are you doing out here?"

I spent an hour of quality time with Jen, getting the whole story (I thought) before walking her back to town. Neither of us could figure out what to do about the car. The broader trail went dead on both ends and there wasn't a chance we'd be able to drive it down the single-file path back to town. It was possible that a clear course existed somewhere, but I was damned if I knew where.

As soon as we reached the PD, I sat Jen down by the phone and had her call her family. While she did that I told Al to beep German and I went to the bathroom to wash my face and arms with cool water. I almost didn't care about finding Jason's trail; Jen's story had proved even more interesting than our elusive legend.

Mrs. Jackson and Jen's children arrived almost immediately and all of them pounced on Jen, smothering her with sloppy kisses and questions. When Billy arrived, he had to fight his way through the mob to clasp his wife's hand and ask her tearfully if she was okay. It touched my heart to see his freshly combed and still-damp hair, and the clean shirt he wore with oil-stained pants.

I wouldn't let Jen speak a word of explanation until German arrived. By that time, of course, everyone in the room had begun to exhibit mild hostility toward me, but Jen took my side by telling them, "I'd just as soon tell it once and be done."

German strode into the room twenty minutes later, pleased to find that he had an excuse to lounge around the air-conditioned PD for a while. With Jen and her children plopped into all the available chairs, we noncivilians had to lean against the desk.

"I was driving along the highway," Jen began, "going to get some milk because the kids like to have cereal for breakfast. And I noticed there wasn't much traffic on the road, but I just figured, you know, it's kinda late and everybody's already home."

She told the story with the simple calm of a mother who has lulled many a child to sleep with tales of frogs and princes. Having already heard this particular story, I was listening for deviations from the version she'd told me earlier.

"So I was just driving along and thinking about what to cook for dinner the next day, and then the engine went dead. Like that time it was the alternator?" She looked at Billy, who nodded his remembrance. "I coasted over to the side of the road and I wasn't sure what to do next, because there weren't any houses around and I didn't especially want to go traipsing along the road at night."

"Exactly where was this?" German asked.

"Out on the highway, just before I got to the river," Jen said.

"Nobody reported a disabled vehicle, did they?" German asked me.

"Nope. Let her finish." I could tell he was going to try assigning the usual procedure to Jen's highly unusual experience.

"Anyway, before I could really think about what to do, I saw this bright light coming at me. And I thought, well good, that trucker can help me out. But pretty quick I knew it was too bright to be headlights. I could see it was coming from up above me and then I thought it might be a rescue helicopter, so close to the river and all. Maybe looking for a lost fisherman?"

"I haven't heard about any rescue teams being out," German said importantly.

I shushed him. "Go ahead," I told Jen. "Take your time."

So far her story, while not word for word, was the same as when I'd first heard it. Jen seemed to be telling us the events exactly as they'd transpired. I recalled that she'd been president of the drama club in high school, and that her acting ability won her the leading role in three plays.

"Well, this light started to blink, like it was sending out a message. And then it—oh, I don't know. I guess you could say it danced. After that I passed out."

There was a moment of expectant silence as Jen looked at the concerned faces around her. Even the children were keeping still, subdued by their mother's calm demeanor.

"When I woke up," Jen went on, "I was on board a spaceship, and there were these beings all around me."

I heard German snort, as I'd expected he would. Al and I managed to remain professionally detached.

"Aliens kidnapped you?" Billy asked. He'd been holding onto his wife's hand for dear life, but that was no longer enough. He got down on his knees in front of her, wrapped his arms around Jen's waist and looked into her eyes. "Are you all right, honey? Did they hurt you?"

Jen placed a reassuring hand on his shoulder. "No, sweetie. They didn't hurt me. They just wanted to tell me some stuff I'd forgotten about. They told me I have a mission to complete here on Earth."

"Didn't I tell you?" Mrs. Jackson shot to her feet

and threw her hands in the air as if the hallelujah spirit had been injected into her soul. "My little Jen has a mission, you hear? I always said she was special! There ain't nothing ordinary about my girl!"

"Now, Mama, I wish you'd calm down before your blood pressure gets up," Jen advised.

"Calm down? I don't believe I'll ever be calm again!" Mrs. Jackson's eyes sparkled and her face glowed a healthy rose color. Had anyone wandered in at that moment he'd have thought Mrs. Jackson's only child had single-handedly won the Super Bowl. "Now, Jennie, you tell us—what is this mission?"

That was a question I hadn't bothered to ask, preoccupied as I'd been with the mystery of the car on the trail. I assumed the answer would involve the words peace and mankind. Possibly love.

"It's the funniest thing," Jen said, almost to herself. "Deep down, I always knew it. I felt it, but I guess I needed to be reminded. It wasn't like they put it in words—as a matter of fact, they didn't use words at all. They communicated with my mind. You know . . ." She smiled at Billy. "The way you do sometimes."

That brought a grit-eating grin to Billy's face, and I fervently hoped no one would ask for specifics. Mrs. Jackson was tapping her foot, impatient with Jen's unnecessary asides, and Al and German were observing the show with amusement.

"It's just what I've been doing," Jen went on. "My mission is to have babies, just like these." She tucked her free arm around the nearest child and gave it an affectionate squeeze.

"That's ridiculous!" Mrs. Jackson's mood went

from elation to disgust in a split second. "That's not a mission, it's just carelessness! There's nothing special about bringing kids into the world. Now, Jen, I know you're meant for more than that. They came for you because you're special. They must've told you something else."

Jen drew herself in and folded her hands in her lap. "They did, Mama." She bit her lip, preparing to deliver news that she clearly did not think her mother wanted to hear.

Oh, my word, I thought. She's pregnant with an alien's baby! Which only goes to show my psychic powers aren't all they could be.

"They told me I'm one of them." Jen spoke so quietly I almost didn't hear.

"What?" Billy and Mrs. Jackson asked.

"Cool!" proclaimed one of the children, and the other two caught the mood.

"Awesome!"

"You're an alien, Mom?"

"Did you see Mr. Data on the spaceship?"

"You don't look like an alien." The logical-minded tot reached out to touch the bridge of Jen's nose. "Where's your wrinkles?"

"Hush up, all of you!" Mrs. Jackson's face turned a brighter red and her arms were locked together across her chest like impenetrable armor. "Now, Jennifer Ann Jackson, you stop talking nonsense about aliens and spaceships, and tell me where you've been!"

Oh ho. The ultimate symptom of Mother Wrath! Mrs. Jackson had pulled out her unruly daughter's full maiden name. I wanted to point out that she'd been perfectly happy with the UFO story when it made Jen—and by extension, Mrs. Jackson—look like a Very Important Person. The tale was less appealing now that it seemed Jen was a Very Important Klingon and Mom was, well, not Mom.

"I'm sorry, Mama, but it's true. They explained it all while I was on the ship. I'm one of them—the Celenians, they're called. We come from a planet twelve light-years from here."

"Just hush!" Mrs. Jackson ordered.

Jen shook her head. "You have to hear. I know it's not fair. You've raised me and I'll always love you and think of you as my mother. The truth is, though, that I was traded for your real daughter just after she was born. The real Jennifer—"

"I'm not listening, I'm not listening!" Mrs. Jackson put her hands over her ears and continued chanting the denial.

"The real Jennifer," Jen repeated, a little louder, "is living on Celenia, and she says to tell you hello and that she's real happy."

"Now, wait a minute." Billy's face showed the strain of trying to sort through his wife's revelations. "If the real Jen is on some other planet, am I married to you or to her?"

Jen cupped his chin lovingly in her hand. "You're married to me, honey. You've never even met the real Jennifer. But my name is Seria. Jennifer has her own family back on Celenia. She's got the same mission I've got—to have babies. See, you and me, Billy, have these little ones that belong to both worlds. That's how the universe will get to be one big, happy family. There's a lot of us, spread out to all the planets, and all of us marrying and having babies with the best men. In the end, we'll create one mixed-together race that can live in peace."

I just knew peace would enter into it somewhere.

"Mrs. Atwater," German said finally, "how much had you been drinking before you saw the light?"

"My Jen's no drunk!" Mrs. Jackson stopped chanting long enough to defend the family honor.

"Yes, ma'am," German agreed, "but this isn't your Jen. Your Jen is on some planet out there, shacked up with a prime specimen of alien manhood."

"How dare you?" Mrs. Jackson was no longer sure just who or what she was defending.

"Are you still Mommy?" the oldest child asked.

"I sure am, Bubby," Jen said. She planted a kiss on the worried youngster's head.

"Everybody just get hold of yourselves!" Mrs. Jackson insisted. "Jen's my daughter, just like she's always been, and I can't believe anybody's paying attention to this crap."

"You'll come to accept it in time," Jen promised her. "I know it's hard for you."

"The important thing is that Jen's okay." Billy, in his simpleminded logic, had gone right to the heart of it. "Now let's gather everybody up and go home."

"Wait, wait!" I said, reluctant to let the entertainment leave. "Tell them about the car!"

"Oh, that." Jen was not and never had been overly concerned about her stranded vehicle. "My people aren't very good at reading maps. I guess that explains why I'm always getting lost. Anyway, they meant to send me and the car right back where they found me, but they didn't quite make it. It's stuck out there in the woods, Billy, and I don't know how we'll get it out."

"Don't worry about that," Billy assured her. "If an alien can get it stuck, I reckon a red-blooded earthling can get it loose."

"There's no aliens and they didn't put your car in the woods!" Mrs. Jackson shouted.

"Ma'am, if you don't quiet down, I'll have to—"

We never learned what German would have to do. When Mrs. Jackson threw her purse at him, he ducked, then came back fighting.

"That's it!" he announced. "Mrs. Jackson, I'm charging you with assault on an officer."

"Go to hell!" Mrs. Jackson scooped up her purse and stormed out the door.

"Best just to let her go," Jen advised. "You can see she's having trouble getting used to the idea of me being Seria. When she calms down, I'm sure she'll apologize to you."

German grunted, but made no attempt to halt Mrs. Jackson's departure. I thought he ought to slap her with every violation he could think of, but when I turned to say so, I realized it was hopeless. German was staring glassy-eyed at Jen, apparently half convinced by her quiet confidence and afraid to take on whatever alien powers she possessed.

"You ready to go, Jen? I mean, Seria?" Billy asked. He helped his wife to her feet, hoisted the smallest child onto his shoulders, and herded the interspecies family out the door.

"Which one of you wants to write this up?" Al asked with a wicked grin.

"Happened on German's shift," I reminded him. "I'm going home to take a shower."

On my way down the street I pondered the questions that had yet to be answered. Were Billy and Jen/Seria legally married? How would his family feel about having an alien daughter-in-law? Did marriage to Billy give Jen/Seria citizenship on Earth? Most of all, though, I worried that the Celenians had sent us an ambassador specifically told to mate with a prime Earth specimen, and they hadn't chastised her for choosing Billy.

It was the worst possible combination—Wayne was working day shift while I worked evenings. That meant he'd be heading for home just as I went on duty. Worse still, my morning was usually barren without him.

For lack of a better way to kill a few hours, I lingered in the shower until all the hot water was gone. I used a blow dryer on my hair, and in an act of pure desperation, I tweezed my eyebrows. No one would recognize me in my well-groomed condition.

By the time I'd finished dressing, it was two P.M., leaving me an hour in which to do nothing. I'm not averse to lounging when the world has quietly settled down for a spell, but the excitement of meeting a real live space alien had revved my adrenaline. There wasn't a chance of taking a quiet nap, and there seemed no place to go but work.

"You're way early," Al said when he saw me in full uniform.

"I know. I was getting stir crazy. What I really want to do is get back out to the woods and pick up

Jason's trail, but if I'm not right here at shift change, German will have a fit." I flopped into the extra chair and twiddled my thumbs.

"Well, I found out about that soldier for you," Al said proudly.

I sat up straighter, optimistically waiting to hear the news about Vanessa's father. Ever mindful of the fragility of my control over Al, I reinforced it with a grateful smile. "You did? So soon? Al, you really are a treasure. I'd be lost without you here."

Seemed to me like I'd laid it on a little thick, but Al was oblivious. A few more kind words from me and he'd have purred.

"Were you able to get James McCrary's current address?" I asked slyly.

"Arlington Cemetery, most likely," he said. "The boy's been dead a long time. Since about 1966, if I understood correctly." He gave me a puzzled look. "You mean that's not what you expected?"

"Yes, it's exactly what Marty told me. I was hoping—I don't know. That James McCrary would turn out to be alive and wanted in twelve states for murder."

Al shifted his considerable weight and pondered how to word his next question. He finally fixed on, "Kay, you're not looking for some crazy way to get that Hyland girl off, are you?"

"Of course not. But I *am* open to the possibility that someone else killed Meredith. After all, Al, Vanessa is innocent until a jury convicts her. It seems to me we ought to investigate every lead, just to be sure."

A smug little grin flashed across his face before he

could stop it. Shaking his head, Al said, "You never learn. Every time something like this happens, you start feeling sorry for the worst kind of people."

"I never feel sorry for killers, Al. I just—"

"You still writing letters to that serial killer in prison?"

I stuttered a bit before I could explain. "I don't feel *sorry* for killers," I repeated. "I have a great deal of sympathy for the Bradleys, and for Vanessa's adoptive family, too. What's more, I believe in the integrity of the law, which means I feel compelled to thoroughly examine—"

"You sure get defensive about it, don'tcha? I think it's real nice that you're so softhearted."

There's no reasoning with Al when he gets on a track, so I didn't even try. Instead I pulled out the thick file on Vanessa we'd gotten from the TBI and reread every boring detail. Then I reread my own report about the night Meredith had been murdered, and finally I closed my eyes and played back the scene as I remembered it. It was a stray remark from the Tea Room opening that puzzled me, and by the time German arrived to hand over the beeper, I was raring to go.

Doc James had a waiting room full of coughing, hacking, sneezing, wheezing patients who probably blew extra germs my way when the receptionist relayed Doc's permission for me to join him right away.

"This is official business, right?" he asked. "You're not sick?"

"Not yet, but it'll be a miracle if I get out of here without catching some fatal disease."

"Fatal, hah!" Doc motioned for me to clear the junk off a chair in the corner and get comfortable. Meanwhile he poured coffee from the stained pot on his desk and offered it to me in a Donald Duck cup. He drank his own from a mug that proclaimed him the WORLD'S BEST DADDY.

Once the place had been designer perfect, but Doc James worked it hard. The formerly mauve carpet was closer to puce, and the potted plant in the window had been dead for ages. Custom-built bookshelves that had once held artful arrangements of artwork now suffocated under the weight of medical volumes, stray papers, and an assortment of papier-mâché knickknacks, most likely donated by Doc's grade school sons. Frankly, I liked the office much better with Doc and his personality in it.

I set my coffee on top of a stack of magazines, not able to so much as sip at the vile black liquid Doc had brewed. "You're paid so well," I said. "Why don't you hire a cleaning woman?"

"Tried it once," he said shortly. "She moved everything."

"Well, I don't want to keep you from your humanitarian duty. I just need a few minutes of your time, and you're welcome to bill the city. I doubt you'll get paid, but go ahead and try."

"I should pay you," he said. "For rescuing me from the sniffling hoard. Do you know how many people have thrown up on me today?"

"You have a very bad attitude," I pointed out.

"Our last doctor was an absolute angel. Thoughtful, caring, compassionate. Even made house calls."

"So I've heard," Doc said meaningfully. He'd heard the tale of his promiscuous predecessor. "But he isn't here, is he? I'm all you have, unless you'd all like to charter a bus and take your aches and pains to Dr. Perfect. Wherever he is."

"Maybe you should lay off the caffeine," I suggested. "I really do need some information, though. About Vanessa Hyland."

"You'll get nothing from me, my dear. Kick me, shoot me, beat me with a rubber hose. Doctor-patient confidentiality binds me." He drank the last of the coffee in his cup and refilled it from the pot. "Next question."

"I wasn't going to ask about Vanessa specifically. Let me finish, okay? The night of the murder, she'd been to the Med Center to get Demerol for a headache. The TBI looked into it, and according to their report, you gave it to her."

"She had a killer headache," he said straight-faced.

"Her sister-in-law mentioned to me that the combination of Demerol and her regular medication really knocks Vanessa for a loop. Now in the report it says she takes Tegretol. All I want to ask you is, what's Tegretol and what's it for? Is it a tranquilizer or something?"

Doc poked his tongue into his cheek and seemed to be pondering his answer. Finally he said, "Is this part of the case against Vanessa Hyland?"

"I don't know," I told him truthfully. "That's why I'm asking you about this drug. You can bet the TBI will know what it's for, but I don't have a medical expert on my team. I'm wondering if it could have an effect on Vanessa's behavior."

"Tegretol is an anticonvulsant," he said sharply. "It's used to control seizures."

"Seizures? You mean Vanessa has epilepsy? Good heavens!" I was stunned, although for the life of me I couldn't have said why. It wasn't as if I thought epilepsy was a visible disease.

"No, dear," Doc said patronizingly. "She isn't crazy."

"I never thought she was." Well, I'd wondered if she might be a psychopath, but that had nothing to do with her epilepsy.

"Didn't you?" He was genuinely skeptical.

"Look, Doc, I just came in here to find out if Tegretol might have caused Vanessa to commit a crime and then forget she'd done it."

He relaxed a bit, even looked a little ashamed of himself for overreacting. "Sorry. The general public's knowledge of TLE is—"

"TLE?"

"Temporal Lobe Epilepsy. Most people are frightened of those who have it, whether they know anything about it or not. And usually they're completely ignorant."

"But they can do some sort of surgery to fix epilepsy, can't they?" I asked. "Why wouldn't Vanessa have had that done?"

"You're extraordinarily nosy, Miss Martin," Doc said. "There's a cure for that. Why don't we slice open your brain right now and fix you?"

He'd made his point, to a degree. "Nosiness doesn't affect my life—"

"You'd be surprised. And TLE often has very little effect on its victims. Especially with medication."

He certainly knew more about the subject than I, and there was good reason to believe him. Vanessa had never exhibited any symptoms, and she'd been exposed to all sorts of public attention since she'd come to town. She'd attended church and quite a number of community gatherings, plus she'd worked full-time at the lumber store. "If she'd had a seizure, we'd all know about it by now," I mused aloud.

"Not necessarily," Doc corrected. "TLE seizures can last for as little as a few seconds and consist of nothing more than a blank stare."

"Really? I thought there were—I don't know. Bouts of violent behavior."

"In some cases," Doc conceded. "There are a multitude of symptoms, ranging from a tingling sensation all the way to complete unconsciousness. Automatisms, which means repeating the same action over and over again. Amnesia—forgetting the episode entirely. Hallucinations, both visual and auditory and sometimes even olfactory."

"Wait, wait." I held up my hand to stop him. "You mean someone with Temporal Lobe Epilepsy might see visions and hear voices?"

Doc nodded eagerly, happy that he'd been able to educate me. "Yes. It's also common for the person to smell odors that aren't there."

"So Joan of Arc may have had epilepsy?" I asked.

"I'd never thought of it, but that's a possible

explanation. It's equally possible that she was a prophet, chosen by God. Take your pick."

Doc, of course, didn't understand why I'd asked about Joan of Arc, but that was okay. At least pieces were starting to come together in my mind, even if the picture hadn't yet become clear.

"And while Vanessa—or some hypothetical person—is having a seizure complete with hallucinations, might that person commit a crime without even realizing it? And then forget it afterward?"

"Unlikely," Doc said firmly.

"Why?"

"You're taking an extremely broad spectrum of symptoms and trying to pick and choose the ones you like. Before you convict on the basis of a slight abnormality, you'd better spend some time with a neurologist. Getting the facts. And then remember that a blanket statement about TLE won't necessarily apply to the individual."

He stood up to signal that it was time for me to leave. I followed suit, but I was determined to make one thing clear before he threw me out.

"I'm not saying Vanessa is guilty just because she has epilepsy. It surprised me to learn that, yes. And you're right; I don't know a thing about this."

He put a hand on my shoulder and walked me down the hallway to his waiting room. "I jumped all over you, didn't I? Sorry. Rough day."

I thought we were friends again, but before I could get Doc to confirm it, he was pounced upon by an urchin with a runny nose.

"Pretty Polly!" Doc boomed.

"Doc, Doc!" Polly replied. And then she vomited all over his shoes.

Leaving Doc and his receptionist to handle the aftermath, I headed back to the job. I was already on the sidewalk before I thought of another question I should have asked: could epileptic hallucinations include visions of spaceships and alien beings?

CHAPTER

10

I CERTAINLY WOULD HAVE PREFERRED TO ride my way back into the woods, but if there was any hope of catching up to Jason, I'd have to sneak in on foot. Once again, Sun's schedule would be disrupted and I was to blame. I promised my guilt monitor I'd give him a special treat later to make up for my negligence.

I retraced my steps along the trail, hoping the sunlight would hold out until I could get back to the spot where I'd found the oil leak. Given a choice, I'd have gone directly there, but German had ordered me to look over Jen's car one more time. He was quite taken with his temporary power.

When I came to the wide intersecting trail, I stopped to think over my options. If I walked right past and took up Jason's oil trail, German would never know. I'd already told him there was no way I could see of getting that car into the woods without breaking branches and leaving indentations in the ground. I didn't recall seeing any evidence to suggest that the car had gotten there by any means other than Jen had described.

I turned to the right to satisfy my own curiosity,

not German's command. Naturally, I didn't believe space aliens had transported Jen's car from the highway to the woods without so much as an avenue in between. When I'd responded to her emergency signal earlier, I had been on the lookout for obvious signs of distress—blood, severed limbs, like that. How was I to know I should have been dodging laser beam sensors or photon torpedoes?

The battered Chevy sat just where we'd left it in the dead center of the clearing. It looked innocent enough. I circled the perimeter slowly, searching the ground for tire tracks. If I could figure out the direction Jen had come from, maybe I could start piecing together the real story.

Twice around the clearing and I found nothing! I wrote it off to heavy leaf buildup—pine needle mulch is springy and had probably bounced back after the car passed. Obviously the car had been driven into the woods, but damned if I could find its path.

The Chevy, though, would surely hold a clue. First I checked the tires for traces of dirt or leaf mold, but the only things stuck in the tread were the usual chert and a few blobs of hot mix. Odd, I thought, but I still wasn't convinced. Only puzzled. One thing I'd learned from my quick inspection— the planning and execution of this practical joke had taken a quicker mind than I possessed.

Opening the driver's door carefully, I scanned the front seat and made a mental note of the loose items I found there—an open pack of gum, one shoe of a size to fit a toddler, a half-eaten snack box of raisins. I checked the odometer to assure myself that it did not register light-years. It had rolled over at least once, possibly twice, and I gave Billy Atwater extra points for working his miracles on the old clunker to keep it running.

The backseat was home to a child's car safety seat and an assortment of travel toys, but no asteroid chunks. I ran my hand under the driver's seat and found a flashlight; under the passenger's seat I found a G.I. Joe action figure, less arms, and a half-dozen hairpins.

It was stifling hot inside and I could feel sweat beading on my forehead. Was it worth the trouble? I asked myself.

Crawling out backward, I stood and stared at the car, thoroughly stumped. No tracks, no traces, no clues. The trees surrounding the clearing were spaced, at most, two feet apart, and none seemed to bear signs of having been pushed aside to allow the Chevy to pass.

I slammed the car's door shut and rubbed my sweaty palms on my pants. How that car got into that spot was a mystery to me, and I congratulated Jen on her ingenuity. Sooner or later we'd find out where she'd been during the forty-eight hours or so she'd been missing, and why she'd concocted the outlandish story of alien abduction. Until then my report would reflect the facts and I wouldn't waste any more valuable time dwelling on the case of the incredible car.

I made sure the windows were rolled up, but left the doors unlocked as Jen had done earlier, then turned to leave. Immediately I was smacked in the face by a thick and rubbery web spun between two saplings. I rubbed at it absently, knowing it wouldn't be my only arachnid encounter of the day.

The pesky web reminded me of something, though. I made another circle around the car, looking closely at the grille, the windows, the antenna. Impossible, I thought, but a single check assured me it was true. There wasn't a single spiderweb attached to Jen's car. What's more, none of the hairy little beggars were crawling on or near it.

There'd been no spiders or flies inside, either. If aliens had sprayed it with a radioactive repellent, it was darned sure working. I'd have to arrange to have myself abducted.

Heading back toward the main trail, I felt my heart rate increase in anticipation of picking up Jason's scent. Oh please, I prayed to any deities who happened to be listening, let the oil leak be a strong one. Let there be large and regular drops that lead right to the front door of his lair. As an afterthought I added, And let me be quicker and stronger than he is.

In spite of the humidity, I moved along at a good clip. Normally I'm not a superstitious woman, but history had taught me that when it seems all your fondest dreams are about to come true, the alarm clock rings. I crossed fingers on both hands and tried to pretend I didn't expect to find Jason.

I'd noticed that the light had grown dimmer, but assumed it was due to the overhang of heavy foliage. Trudging along toward the site of Jason's accident, though, I paid closer attention to the sky. Lo and behold, it looked as if a storm might be moving in—just in time to save threatened crops and destroy any signs of Jason's trail.

Feeling the first tremors of panic, I moved faster along the path, paying little attention to the surroundings. By the time I reached the spot where Jason and his bike had gone down, my heart was pounding like a bass drum on a caffeine high.

I dropped to my knees and searched for the oil spill, half expecting it to have disappeared. I almost cried with relief when I found it right away, then began to worry all over again as I heard the rumble of distant thunder.

Ten minutes later, after examining the ground and every leaf on it, I found the first dime-sized drop of oil. Locating it dashed my hopes rather than bolstering them. What had I been thinking? I asked myself angrily. There was no chance I'd be able to follow the tiny drops, not if each one hid in and among fallen leaves and branches the way the first one had.

I stood up and dusted off the dirt and leaves clinging to my clothes. The best I could hope for was that Jason had stayed on the path and that no other intersected it. I'd followed the woodland trail, keeping my eyes on the ground. It wasn't likely I'd find a useful sign, but having come so far, I refused to give up without a fight.

With considerably less enthusiasm than I'd had before, I continued through the woods, eyes down on the off chance I'd find a big red arrow with Jason's name on it. He might have lost some chrome, I said to encourage myself. All sorts of loose pieces could have fallen off his bike after the accident.

From far across the river I heard Thor laughing at my fantasies.

The trail twisted back and forth like a drunken snake, but it seemed to me that it was leading me back toward the west. I'd never ridden the section of trail I was on because of the narrow trenches and extremely low branches. The overhang wouldn't be a problem for Jason on a bike, of course, but Sundance was far taller than a motorcycle.

Here and there I spotted fresh breaks in the tender limbs and I promised myself they'd been made by Jason. Perhaps this wasn't just a trail, but his driveway. It could lead straight to him.

All of this, of course, was nonsense and I knew it, but after so many months of tracking him, losing him, being sneered at by him, I was beginning to lose my mind along with faith in myself, and I was determined not to let another setback take away my spirit, too.

Thunder didn't necessarily mean rain. I was not necessarily on a fool's mission.

The sky had grown darker, almost dusklike, but I was afraid to use my flashlight. As sure as I did that, Jason would be there and the beam would alert him to my presence.

I knew I'd be going home in the dark, having to step slowly and carefully, and that I'd probably end up with a new collection of scrapes and bruises. I kept moving, heading more directly toward the west and hoping I'd be able to stay on the nearly obscured trail in the darkness.

And then I saw the dogleg. An equally narrow path split off to my left. It could have taken me back to the east or it might twine itself around for a while and head into the woods in any direction at all. I stopped, feeling disoriented and hopeless. There was no sense in continuing, I told myself.

On the other hand, it had been several minutes since I'd heard thunder, and there might be time to investigate both trails. What to do?

A gentle breeze had been building, and I opened my top button to let the cool air refresh me. The unmistakable scent of rain was in the air, along with something else. Wood smoke!

Straight ahead on the path I'd been following, someone was burning dry wood! I took off at a near jog, now deliriously happy that the storm was moving in. Without the low clouds and slight breeze, the smell of smoke would have gone straight up, instead of wafting through the twittering leaves to me.

A few hundred yards along I spotted the glow from a small campfire and came to a complete halt. For a moment I experienced a disturbing sense of déjà vu. Hadn't I done this before?

The campfire in the darkness—oh, yes! I remembered it well. The last time I'd gone chasing after that falsely promising beacon, I'd come into the woods from the west side of town, down River Road and past the old Tyler place. I still had no idea where I was exactly, but I was fairly sure I'd found my way back to the satanists' gathering place.

It didn't surprise me in the least that Jason would be one of them. He was probably their leader. That should turn a few people around, I thought smugly. Just wait until all the kind souls in Jesus Creek find

out they've been feeding and defending the Anti-
christ himself!

Moving as carefully and quietly as I could, I
stepped closer, lurking behind the large tree trunks
that shielded me from the satanists and them from
me. Finally I was close enough to hear voices,
although I couldn't make out the words.

I moved like a snake, silent and sure, getting
closer and braver until I was huddled behind a
giant oak on the very edge of their unholy circle.
The scene was just as I remembered it from years
before—a nicely blazing fire inside a circle of stones,
and ten or twelve robed figures, their faces obscured
by attached hoods.

Most of them were sitting on fallen logs, although
a couple had thoughtfully brought along folding
lawn chairs for comfort. On the far edge of the small
clearing was a red and white Coleman cooler, and I
deduced from the picnic in progress that it con-
tained beer and ice. I supposed it would later serve
as an altar for their evil rituals.

Individual conversations were going on and I
strained to hear the one nearest me. The words
weren't entirely clear but the gist of it seemed to be
that somebody's expletive-deleted boss was an
expletive deleted. Satanic code, I thought, and
nearly giggled.

They'd roasted meat, probably over the open fire,
and the aroma made my stomach sit up and beg. I
watched them gorging on hunks of the stuff, eating
with their hands and washing it down with Bud.

The casual feast went on until my legs burned
from the squatting position I'd assumed. I didn't

dare sit—I wanted to be on my feet in case they
brought in a sacrificial victim who needed my help.

Finally, a big old fat guy in a grease-stained robe
tossed his empty beer can to the ground and took
center stage by the fire.

"Boys!" He called them to attention with an
authoritative voice. "We've got some weather coming
in on us, so we'd better get started."

What? I thought. You can't call on your dark
powers to stop the rain?

"Brother Carter, give us your report."

Another, much slighter member of the group
stood and joined the leader by the fire. He looked
up, apparently to see if the rain had started falling
yet—rather like a turkey, I thought—and his filthy
hood fell away.

I couldn't hold back my startled gasp but a close
thundering rumble covered it. The little demon was
Scott Carter, a local teen who'd tangled with the
law in minor ways on several occasions. Scott and I
had a history, and I wouldn't have been at all surprised to learn that he was our elusive Jason. I
wasn't entirely stunned, now that I thought about
it, to find him mingling with that bunch.

"I been all over town with 'em, Brother Johnson,"
Scott said proudly.

Brother Johnson? Could it possibly be that the
head of the cult was Dave Johnson?

That was not only unexpected, it was disap-
pointing. Dave and his wife Martha had organized
Bible study classes for the local youth. They spon-
sored dances and potlucks, always with a Christian
theme. More importantly, though, Dave Johnson

had helped me out of a sticky situation during my last encounter with the satanists.

"Sometimes I stick around to watch their faces," Scott went on. He hadn't bothered to replace his hood, and I could see the smart-aleck sneer. "Lots of times they turn right around and show that flyer to their women!"

A group groan expressed appalled disapproval. Brother Johnson raised a hand to quiet them.

"Now, brothers. This is the very reason we're here. Our weak brothers have been brainwashed, and it's up to us to return them to the path of manhood."

Wait a minute, I said to myself. They aren't satanists, they're—

"The Brotherhood of Strength is charged with the burden of setting right what's gone wrong!" Brother Johnson sermonized. "The Lord has given us examples to follow, and families nowadays are ignoring that. Women go out to work, men get conned into doing women's chores, and that weakens us all! Foreigners and lesbians have twisted us all around."

I wanted to ask if he had particular foreigners in mind, or just those foreign to Jesus Creek.

"Our weak brothers are afraid. They run from their women and they'll run from what is right. We've got to bombard them from all sides if they're ever gonna get it through their heads that they have been turned into slaves!"

Oh, how I wished Delia could have been there. Roger, too. He'd have marched right in, told them how very right they were, and somehow convinced

them to stitch up a gross of frilly aprons for their
next fund-raiser. I, unfortunately, was so amused I
couldn't have spoken without giggling. I'd already
had to cram my fist into my mouth to prevent a
chuckle.

Thunder rolled, lightning flashed, and the Brothers
glanced nervously at their watches. I wanted to see
the other faces, but there was no hope of that. Idiocy,
sad to say, isn't against the law, so I couldn't very well
barge in and flash my badge.

"We've got to take back the rights that make us
men!" Johnson said. "And we've made a start!" He
indicated a lump of fur on the edge of the clearing.

I strained for a better look and finally identified
the lump as a deer carcass.

"Some of you have already fought a battle for this
basic right! Blood has been shed in defense of our
manly strength!"

A chill ran through me as realization dawned.
The deer they'd just killed and eaten had been
taken out of season, but that wasn't the blood Dave
Johnson was referring to. The game warden who'd
been shot months earlier—there'd been some question about how any hunter could have mistaken his
blaze orange gear for an animal. I knew as surely as
I was standing there that the Brotherhood of
Strength had killed him, and not accidentally.

It was with fear and trembling that I eased away
from the clearing, prepared to return to town, when
Dave Johnson interrupted his oratory to ask, "What
was that?"

It was my beeper.

The attending membership of the Brotherhood of

Strength turned and looked toward the woods. I toyed with the idea of remaining perfectly still, hidden like a deer, but the beeper's tone was so clear and high-pitched there was no question they'd heard it. They all started shuffling toward my position, emboldened by alcohol and macho numbers.

I shot up and took my first running step in the same instant. A blinding flash of lightning gave me enough light so that I could see the trail I'd come in on and be sure I was following it out. Unfortunately, it also allowed my pursuers to get a good look at the quarry and know they weren't chasing an irritable grizzly or even a three-headed Martian—just one very frightened, uppity female.

At our last encounter they'd been friendly and helpful, but this time I'd actually been spying on them, and they had good reason to want their activities kept secret. I had to assume they were smart enough to know I'd spill my guts to NOW, if not to the homicide squad. The certain knowledge that they would kill me just as easily as they'd killed the game warden kept me moving. If they'd already killed once to hide their illegal hunting, they'd have no hesitation about killing again to protect themselves from a murder charge.

My feet flew! I could have outdistanced Sundance, even stumbling over brush and fallen branches the way I was, and still it felt as if I were running in place.

I could hear huffing and puffing and grunting behind me, with an occasional bit of swearing whenever one of them fell. It struck me that they'd have done better to remove those cumbersome robes before they lit out after me. Women, of course, would instinctively have hiked the skirt out of the way, but had the men thought of doing that?

Behind me the stomping and pounding fell away as I left them in the darkening woods—except for one pair of feet that kept pace and sounded to be no more than a yard back. I wanted to look back and see if that one had hiked his skirt. I wanted to ask why the hell they were wearing skirts in the first place.

My questions would have to wait. Another crack of thunder opened the heavens and rain poured down from vats. I was drenched in half a minute and the leaves beneath my feet turned slick and scummy. The roar of the downpour drowned out footsteps and I had no idea where my pursuer was until I felt a hand on my shoulder.

I jerked away and threw every ounce of energy and fear I had into escape. Trees and logs were dark shapes that leaped out at me from the hazy gloom. I didn't know where I was, but I knew it was unlikely I'd managed to stay on the trail. There was no hope of getting back to town, where I could find help. I'd have to keep running aimlessly until the man behind me collapsed—or I did.

I slipped on a slick patch of mud and went sprawling to the ground on my stomach. Pushing myself up, I was knocked flat again by the impact as he barreled into me and went down himself. Through the rain and my panic I could just make out the face of Scott Carter.

Figures, I thought, as I took to my feet just seconds ahead of him. He's young and limber. The old guys are out of breath and cramped up by now. Don't worry about them. Scott's holding a grudge against me, I remembered. He won't quit. And he's lots younger than me, too.

By then my legs were aching and my lungs had started to burn. Rain streamed down my face and trickled into my nose every time I inhaled. I could feel Scott behind me.

His voice was right in my ear when, breathlessly, he muttered, "Bitch cop! You're dead!"

Poor Scott didn't realize that he'd saved my life. In my terror, I'd thought only of escaping from boozed-up nitwits with a homicidal agenda. Scott had just reminded me that I was more than a frightened little woman. I was a bitch cop—with a gun!

I unsnapped the holster as I ran and made sure I had a firm grip on my revolver before pulling it out. Then I darted to the right, held the gun over my head, and fired off three shots before I could regain control of my finger. I saw Scott slide past me as he tried to stop, finally landing hard on his backside.

At last I was in control, although my whole body was shaking. I stepped ahead to stand over Scott and pointed the gun at his head, making sure to keep my trigger finger loose. I didn't want to kill him with a nervous twitch, but I wasn't about to relax my guard, either.

"You're under arrest!" I sounded like a crazed banshee, which annoyed me—I'd rather have appeared to be calm and cool—but it put a healthy fear into Scott. "Get up!" I screamed. "On your feet! Now!"

The boy believed in my power. He hopped to his

feet, looking around frantically for a way to escape. Even Scott, with his limited ability to understand actions and consequences, knew he couldn't outrun a bullet.

"Turn around and start for town!" I ordered. I kept the gun aimed squarely at the back of his head and hoped like hell he wasn't as lost as I was.

It took us nearly two hours to fight our way through the woods and back to civilization. During that time the storm continued to rage, slackening to a drizzle only as we stepped onto the wet, black pavement of Morning Glory Way. Our only exchanges during that time had been Scott's mumbled threats and my manic instructions—"Shut up! Keep walking! I'll blow your head off!"—all delivered in a shrill and piercing squawk.

When we walked into the PD looking like the last refugees of Atlantis, Bill nearly bolted out the back door. I shoved Scott right past him, grabbed the key from its hanger on the wall, pushed Scott roughly into the cell and locked him up tight. I wanted to put my gun down on the desk but found my hand had frozen in place around it. I had to use my left hand to loosen my fingers, and only then did I notice that my right arm ached from carrying heavy lead for so long.

"What happened? Where've you been? Al said he beeped you hours ago and you never checked in. We didn't know what to do!" Bill flapped around in a frenzy.

I already knew they'd been trying the beeper every five minutes. It had grated on my nerves all

the way through the woods and I'd had to fight
myself to keep from pulling it off and throwing it
into a ditch. I was sure the price of a new one would
come out of my salary.

"He's charged with assaulting an officer," I said,
with a glance toward Scott. "Do the paperwork, read
him his rights, get him a lawyer, whatever. I'm
taking off early. Any problems, call Bernie or
German." I slapped the beeper down on Bill's desk.
"Call Mark Warner with the TBI. Tell him the
Brotherhood of Strength may be involved in the
death of that game warden. Scott here is part of
the group. So is Dave Johnson, I think."

I turned and started to slosh my way out before I
remembered. "Why did Al beep me, anyway?"

"Oh," Bill said sheepishly. "We got a call about
another UFO sighting."

I dripped down the street to my little house and
opened the door, hardly daring to believe I was
there. Wayne was enjoying his free evening by
taking in a car show in Nashville, so I couldn't hope
to see him for several more hours. In the meantime,
I pulled off soaking wet socks and shoes and left
them on the rug by the front door along with my
clothes. My hair was plastered to my head and little
rivers dripped from it and ran down my neck and
shoulders. The last thing I wanted to do was crawl
into a tub full of water, but I had a coating of mud
spread all over my body.

It was not a lingering, luxurious bath. It was
functional and warm and it did help me to relax.

Afterward I combed my hair off my face and left it to dry on its own, wrapped up in a lightweight summer robe, and tossed my wet clothes in the sink till they'd stopped dripping.

Fortunately, there was a fresh bag of mini-candy bars in the kitchen. I took chocolate and instant coffee into the living room and stretched my weary legs all the way across the couch. I had just begun to savor the taste of Baby Ruth when the phone rang. Probably Bill, I thought, and considered letting it ring. On the other hand, it could be important. Knowing I'd regret it, I picked up the receiver and said, "Hello."

There was silence on the other end, as if some vinyl siding salesman had forgotten who he'd called and was frantically searching for a name.

"Hello," I said gruffly.

"You think because you made it home you're safe?"

And then there was a click and the dial tone.

I hung up on my end, assuming the caller was a member of the Brotherhood of Strength. If the phone rang again, I'd ignore it. Meanwhile, I decided I'd better clean my gun before it rusted. I got up to get the gun and some oil, and while I was at it, I thought I might as well lock the door and close the curtains.

Nothing to be done about phone calls, I knew. I hadn't recognized the voice, and the only member of the Brotherhood I'd been able to identify was Dave Johnson, who probably didn't do his own dirty work. That's why he was the leader. Pity I didn't have

Caller ID, I thought, so I could return the call and
scare the daylights out of some poor fool who'd think
my woman's intuition was zeroed right in on him
personally.

CHAPTER
11

IF EVER I DESERVED SPECIAL TREATMENT, it was due. Having finally convinced Wayne that I would be perfectly safe on the sidewalks, I dressed for work and sauntered down to Eloise's. The plan called for a massive slab of her breathtakingly delicious chocolate pie—followed by dessert.

Even at midday a few people were roaming about town, dashing from their cars into air-conditioned stores, or just ambling slowly along in an attempt to stay as cool as possible while conducting business that couldn't wait until the cooler evening hours. Most of them waved hello and spoke, and naturally I made every effort to be cheerful in return.

Carrying on as usual isn't easy when everyone you see, when every friend you speak to, is a potential suspect. How did I know Mr. Pate at the hardware store wasn't a member of the Brotherhood of Strength? Was there any way to be sure Ben Jenkins hadn't chased me through the woods and then threatened me by phone?

Throughout the past few years, whenever rumors of satanic cults in our area had surfaced, we'd all imagined the instigators to be formless, faceless invaders, never once supposing that evil could originate within our family. While it was still possible that such was the case, I found myself assuming that missing pets were no more than that, poor crops were a fact of nature, and the satanists were simply a group of insecure men who blamed their failures and unhappiness on the first scapegoats that came to mind.

Foreigners and women. That was vague enough, wasn't it? The Brotherhood of Strength probably vented their frustration out there in the woods, sucking down beer and complaining about their wives. Unfortunately, what had started as mild discontent had escalated to tragic proportions. They'd already targeted a specific victim, assuming the game warden's death had been caused by the Brotherhood. Even if they were innocent of that heinous crime, their flagrant disregard for wildlife law and civil rights did not reassure me. I was determined to put a stop to that lot's activities before they could do any more damage.

Feeling so nervous about associating with longtime friends and neighbors, I declined all offers to join the lingering lunchtime crowd and took a stool at the counter. Eloise knows her customers and what they like, so she had a cup of coffee ready by the time I'd settled into place. Going to the diner is a lot like coming home to Mom's welcoming kitchen.

"It's a miracle you didn't catch your death," she told me sternly.

Eloise not only knows her customers, she manages to keep track of all the events in our lives. Even though Wayne was the only person who'd heard a detailed version of my harrowing evening, I wasn't surprised that Eloise was aware of it and ready to learn more from the source.

A miracle I hadn't caught my death? I wanted to tell her it was a miracle *death* hadn't caught *me*, but I'd decided it was better to make light of the situation. The Brotherhood of Strength didn't need to know how much they'd frightened me. Better to keep them believing I laughed at their incompetence, at least until we could tie them to serious breaches of law and lock them all away.

This did not mean I was going to ignore them. Legally, they were free to gather and drink and hold any opinions they liked. As luck would have it, though, women have learned over centuries of subjugation to take their revenge in devious ways.

"I won't even ask how you found out," I said. "It was the funniest sight, Eloise. I wish you'd been there to see it. If I hadn't been so put off by the rain, I'd have filmed it for one of those *Funniest Videos* programs."

My voice was loud enough so that any interested diners could easily overhear, and I made sure to keep the volume up. I tried to maintain an air of amusement while staying alert to eavesdroppers who might have more than a passing interest in the conversation.

"Funny?" she said. "I'd like to know what was funny about it!"

"Are you kidding? Picture it, Eloise. You've got a bunch of half-drunk men lounging around in choir robes, whining about how their women mistreat them. Brotherhood of Strength? Some of them were strong, all right. I guess their wives have stopped doing laundry." I lowered my voice a notch, as if confiding top secret information. "And you know men are completely hopeless with appliances. Why is it they can't learn to push a few buttons or separate whites from colors?"

Eloise, while she most certainly enjoys the company of men, has little respect for their intelligence. Probably because she married the ones who've never had to use their brains. Bless her heart, Eloise is a sucker for thick black hair and a cleft chin.

"You're telling the truth!" she declared. "I've known scientists who couldn't learn how to empty a vacuum cleaner. Never mind that, though. What about you being chased through the woods and nearly killed?"

Work with me, Eloise. I relaxed my jaw before my teeth could clamp down and took a casual sip of coffee. "It wasn't much of a chase," I explained. "I'd hoped to get them all back to town for questioning, but they gave out on me. Out of shape, I guess. The only one who could keep up with me was the little Carter boy. You know—the kid who's always into some sort of trouble. I guess we all knew he'd come to no good end. Worked out okay, I guess, because we've had some outstanding warrants on him. I don't know if the Brotherhood of Strength is harboring any other criminals or not," I said vaguely.

"They put one of their advertisements on my car the other day," Chester said.

"Oh yeah?" I turned around to face him. "Are you going to join? Dave Johnson's a member. I expect he could vouch for you, in case you have to be recom-

mended. Probably they have some sort of initiation,
too, like crushing beer cans with your teeth."

Chester looked flustered for a moment, until he'd
settled on a strategy. Finally he said, "I don't reckon
I'd better join anything that runs down women. My
wife wouldn't ever let me out of the house to go to
meetings."

The room laughed with him, apparently sincere.
If anyone there was a member, he kept it to himself.

"I don't know, Chet," I warned. "You men had
better stick together on this. Why, before you know
it, we women will be going off to do your jobs and
you'll have to stay home and cook."

There was unanimous agreement on one point—
every man in the room was ready to accept the revolution. A couple expressed concern that they'd never
learn to like lounging around the house, eating bon-
bons and watching soap operas, but their supportive
friends promised to help train them.

Satisfied that my plan to sabotage the Brotherhood of Strength was working nicely, I savored
every bite of my chocolate pie.

Still feeling smug and bolstered by the evident
support of Eloise's clientele, I sauntered down the
street to Proctor's Gas Station. Heat waves rippled
off the pumps, and a family reunion of flies buzzed
around a pool of Orange Crush that had spilled just
outside the door.

Mr. Proctor and Billy Atwater were in the
garage with their heads together over an engine.
As I walked in I felt my stomach clench again,
tightened by the uncertainty of who these two men
really were.

"Hi, fellas!" My voice came out an octave higher than normal and I wished suddenly that I had an icy cold drink to soothe my dry throat.

They both looked up and Mr. Proctor gave me a worried frown. "Little lady, I hear you got yourself in some hot water last night."

"Oh, that." I waved it away.

"That, nothing! Out in the woods, being attacked by ruffians! You got no business being out after dark alone, anyway. I don't know what Reb was thinking when he put you on night shift!" Mr. Proctor pulled a shop rag from his pocket and wiped his hands.

"Yeah, that's right, Kay. The woods out there—well, there's been a lot of strange goings-on." Billy reached for his drink on the workbench and took a swig from the greasy can.

Eager to change the subject, lest one or both of them turned out to be a member of the Brotherhood pumping me for information, I moved to the cluttered table and picked up one of the smaller parts that littered it. "I don't know how you find anything in this mess." I could identify the spark plugs and a fan belt, but most of the other junk could have come from a spaceship, for all I knew.

" 'Please fix,' " I read from a note that was held down by a quart of oil.

"Somebody left it for us," Mr. Proctor explained. "Can't come during regular working hours, they just drop it off here in the shop."

"You don't mean in the shop, surely!" I protested. "Mr. Proctor, you haven't been leaving the place unlocked again after my warning."

"Pshaw," he said. At least, that's what he turned it into. "These locks aren't worth a plug nickel anyway. If somebody wanted to steal, I'd just about be grateful. It's the only way I'm ever gonna get this place cleaned out." He stuck the rag back into his pocket and nodded toward the office. "I'm ready for a break. Come on and I'll buy you a Coca-Cola."

He was taking a break, all right. I saw by the clock on the wall that it was almost time for Mr. Proctor's favorite soap opera. "Thanks anyway, but I want to talk to Billy."

Mr. Proctor didn't seem to mind in the least that I wouldn't be there to share in his afternoon melodrama. He gave me a suit-yourself shrug and toddled away to enjoy televised misery.

"What's up, Kay?" Billy asked with alarm. "It's not Jen, is it? Nothing's happened to her?"

"Calm down, boy!" I ordered before he could get any more upset. "I came by to ask you how she's doing. Any lasting effects from her experience?"

Billy gave it a moment of serious thought. "She seems just like always. Real glad to be back, I guess."

"That's good. And how about you and the kids? Any problems?"

Billy shook his shaggy head. "None now that Jen's back. Seria, that is. Dang! It's hard to remember her name."

"I'll bet it is. Maybe she wouldn't mind if you kept on calling her Jen."

"She says it's kinda important to get used to her real name, because it's time for her to start reconnecting with her people." Billy said this blandly, as if he had no particular feeling about his wife's pronouncement.

"Have you gotten the car back yet?" I asked. I thought if I could learn how the car came out of the woods, I might also discern how it had gotten in.

"You seen that thing?" Billy laughed, as if he found it gently amusing. "I don't know how the heck I'm gonna get that Chevy back to town!"

If Billy had been involved in the scam, he was covering nicely. He seemed genuinely puzzled about how his car had gotten to its present location. "Billy," I said, "tell me the truth. Do you believe space aliens abducted Jen and then plunked your car down in the woods?"

"Well," he said slowly, "it sounds a little far-fetched, but Jen says that's how it happened. I've never known her to lie, especially not about something like this."

"Something like this?" I pounced on his words. "Has Jen tangled with aliens before now?"

"No, of course not. If she had, she'd have mentioned it. I just meant she'd be especially careful to remember this right, what with it being so important and all."

Billy leaned back over the engine he'd been working on when I arrived, satisfied that all the mysteries in his life would reveal themselves in due time. I, however, did not share his faith.

"Look, Billy. It's pretty ridiculous to think that aliens abducted your wife and then put her back in the wrong place. It could be that Jen has problems and needs our help."

He looked up at me without a trace of concern

evident in his face. "It's real nice of you to worry," he told me, "but Jen's doing just fine. She says her people are gonna take care of everything."

On that ominous note I chose to exit.

Eloise had told me that the crime scene tape no longer defaced the Bradley house, so I went directly there from the diner. Marty's car sat in the driveway where it had been since Saturday night. I noticed that Bruce's car was parked beside it, blocking the space Meredith had set aside for customers.

That wouldn't be a problem anymore, I thought. So far as I knew, no one else in the family had a green thumb. It would have been ironic, wouldn't it, if Vanessa had inherited Meredith's talent?

I'd intended to stop for a while at the Bradleys' to assure them that I'd done all I could to help. Saying that, though, would require me to explain that there'd been nothing for me to do because the TBI had arrested the right person. It would take more cruelty than I had in me to throw that undeniable fact into the open, trusting faces of the Bradley family.

I pivoted on my heel and headed straight for the PD. There was a good hour left before my shift began, and I wanted to spend it with Vanessa. She was still being held in the county jail out on Highway 70, and if I borrowed Al's car, I could be there in minutes.

All the time I'd spent thinking about Meredith's murder, I'd tried to devise alternatives to Vanessa's guilt. There was no logical explanation for that. I barely knew the woman, I had no personal interest in her future, and there could be no extenuating circumstances in this case that excused or explained her actions, to allow her the benefit of a doubt.

I had suffered a relapse. My old codependent urges had snuck up on me, and I'd wasted a lot of energy trying to do and believe whatever would make my friends the Bradleys happy. Those of us who suffer from this insidious malady are capable of convincing ourselves of the most outlandish nonsense, and I'd fallen into that trap. I had been feeling extreme guilt because I'd been unable to wish hard enough to make the Bradleys' desires reach fulfillment.

This time when I faced Vanessa, I would do it without preconceived opinions or the pressure of my need to please. I would look at her with wide-open eyes, and I would decide for myself whether I had done enough.

"You don't have to talk to me," I told her flatly. "Or we'll call in your lawyer if you like."

The visiting room at the county jail was a windowless square, decorated like a bus station lobby. Preformed orange plastic hairs stood out against a dust-coated plastic plant. A scratched and dented coffee table salvaged from a low-end trailer park provided a surface for our coffee in cardboard cups.

Vanessa, wearing a neon-orange jumpsuit, sat on one of the chairs, her posture as erect and serene as a queen's. She hadn't touched the coffee in front of her, but neither had she asked for it.

"Mr. Maddox has ordered me not to talk to anybody," she said. "He isn't a trusting man, is he? But I don't see why I shouldn't. What will happen will happen."

"That's a self-destructive attitude," I said. "You've given yourself up to fate, and I don't believe in that. It assumes we aren't responsible for our own actions, or in control of our own lives."

"At the moment," Vanessa said with a look around at her surroundings, "I'm not in control of much. I have power over my reactions to the situation. I have the power of prayer and faith. I intend to use them all. If you think I'll go to prison without a fight, you're mistaken."

There was no defiance in her tone. Her statement was a simple explanation, intended to set me straight.

"Okay, then," I said, hearing a touch of defiance in my own voice, "let's start with the most important question. Not for the record, necessarily, but for my own curiosity. Did you kill Meredith Bradley?"

"No," she said, "I didn't kill my mother."

"Do you know who did?"

"If I had even a suspicion, I'd have mentioned it before now. Remember, Kay—Meredith Bradley was a stranger to me. I don't know who might have held a grudge against her. Our relationship was not only new, but fairly unique. Not even Bruce understands how many blank spaces there were. Or how many full moments."

She was right, of course, that none of us knew how much closeness had developed between Vanessa and Meredith over the past few months. Most likely the motives would be found within those dark valleys that the world would never explore, and Vanessa would be wise to keep to herself whatever resentment she'd felt.

"Meredith added you to her will just before she died," I pointed out. "Why?"

"Because she believed it was a fair thing to do. In spite of her insistence that she'd honestly tried to do the best she could for me, I think there was a grain of guilt about the adoption. I don't have children, but from what I've heard, I'd guess giving away a child is something a mother doesn't forgive herself for."

"*Did* you forgive her?" I asked flatly.

"There was never a question of that. You haven't met my parents. When you do, you'll be impressed. Meredith really did do the best thing for me." Vanessa sounded sincere, but her future depended on her ability to convince us that she had no hard feelings against her biological mother. Facing a murder conviction might turn any of us into an Oscar-winning actress.

"You were the only person in the house when Meredith was killed," I reminded her.

"Except for the person who killed her."

"Are you depending on God to deliver that person to us?" I snapped.

"I wouldn't be surprised if He did," Vanessa said quietly. "You don't depend on God for much, do you?"

"It's the people who pull out His name to appear pious I have questions about."

Vanessa nodded. "Yes, I understand that. I've told you I didn't kill my mother. And now I'll tell you my faith and religious convictions are carefully considered and totally sincere. Both statements are true, but you have the choice of disbelieving either or both."

Clearly the woman in the room with me did not share my codependent weakness. She cared not a whit whether I believed her or liked her. I realized with sickening clarity that I didn't know how to deal with someone that confident.

There didn't seem to be any reason to continue our conversation. D.D. Maddox had nothing to worry about with this client. Her attitude had me thoroughly convinced that she was innocent of the charges against her, in spite of the evidence. I had to conclude that Meredith had been killed by space aliens who had beamed themselves back to the mothership after the crime.

On my way out of the county jail, I met Mark Warner arriving with a briefcase full of paperwork pertaining to the case. I stopped him to ask for an update, even though it was almost time to pick up my beeper and hit the trail again.

"I hear you don't have sense enough to come in out of the rain," he said jovially.

There was no need to pretend with Mark. I filled him in on the few details he'd missed and demanded to be told how he'd heard about the Brotherhood of Strength.

"A good investigator knows everything," he whispered into my ear. "We've been checking on them for a while now. Interrogating witnesses, bugging phones. You know. We're way ahead of you."

One of the deputies watching us through the office window no doubt thought we were exchanging classified information.

"Nobody's going to talk to you!" I said. "You're an outsider."

"I'm a master of disguise. My source thought he—or she—was talking to a founder of this charming colony. You know, you folks oughtn't to be so trusting. Don't believe everything you hear and see; it's not good for you."

He could be right, at that. I'd believed in the invasion of satanists for years, because I thought I'd seen them. Henry and others believed in UFOs. I should learn something from all that, I told myself, and there was one more thing I'd seen with my own eyes that I didn't need to believe in.

"How would you get a car into the woods without leaving a trail?" I filled him in on the details of the Jen Atwater mystery and waited for his expert opinion.

After thinking it over, he said, "You could drop it from a chopper."

"That would attract attention, don't you think?"

Mark shrugged off my objection. "Around here? With UFOs zipping all over the place?"

"I suppose it could have been mistaken for a UFO," I admitted. "But what are the odds people like the Atwaters would go to that much trouble and expense for a practical joke?"

"You ever wonder how much money an abductee can make from the tabloid stories and television appearances?" he asked.

"Well, no. I haven't. That's very clever of you,

Mark. When Jen becomes a national celebrity, her mother will be so proud."

"Do they get the *Enquirer* on Celenia?" he asked. "Of course, there's another way they could've gotten the car in there. You said her husband's a mechanic?"

"Yes." I nodded. "A good one."

"So how long would it take him to dismantle the car and reassemble it in the woods? Not long, I'll bet. Especially if he didn't worry about details. Did the car actually start?"

We hadn't tried the engine. For all I knew, Jen's Chevy didn't even *have* an engine. "I guess that's why you work for the big guys," I said. "Creative thinking."

"I don't get to use my imagination much. Most bad guys walk right into my arms." He pointed a thumb toward the jail. "Like that one."

"After talking to her a few times, I have to say I'm surprised," I admitted. "She seems so bright and . . . composed. Why didn't she cover herself? It would have been easy enough to establish an alibi."

"Maybe she thought we'd never believe she's that stupid. Next thing you know, criminals everywhere will arrange to be found standing over the body with murder weapon in hand. The defense will be, 'But I'm not that stupid.' "

"Relax," I told him. "They aren't that smart, either."

"Oh, yeah? I hear Maddox is already working on a defense based on that very theory."

It wouldn't have surprised me to learn it was true. Maddox is a creative thinker, too.

"I just learned something that may have an impact on the case," I told him. "I expect you've already discovered it, though. Vanessa Hyland has epilepsy."

"You *just* learned that? Good thing for all of us the experts arrived, isn't it? You're right about it affecting the case. It should be clear to any jury that she killed her mother."

I was glad Doc James wasn't there; he'd have ripped Mark into bite-size pieces. The comment sent a flush to my cheeks, too, but I suspected that was because Mark's ignorance mirrored my own.

"Having epilepsy doesn't make her a killer, or even violent," I pointed out. "She takes medication to control the seizures—"

"But she still has them," Mark said. "That's why she can't get a driver's license. She'd have to be free of seizures for at least six months."

"Oh, right!" My temper flared momentarily. "She murdered her mother in cold blood, but she's too ethical to lie to the Department of Transportation! That makes all kinds of sense!"

I could've sworn I saw him flinch, but Mark recovered instantly and gave me a patronizing smile.

"I gather by your passionate defense of Miss Hyland," Mark said in a more serious tone, "that you're not convinced. Still trying to find another suspect?"

"I don't know," I admitted. "I feel like something's not right."

"Sorry to be the one to say this, Kay, but you're famous for being wrong."

He had me there. I rambled on, trying to identify

for myself the source of my gut reaction. "She's so calm about it, and very believable when she says she didn't kill Meredith."

"Uh-huh." Mark patted my head patronizingly. "The jury found Lizzie Borden believable, too."

The previous evening's thunderstorm had washed a summer's worth of dust and grit off leaves, leaving them glistening like jewels in the afternoon sun. Someone had trimmed the Bradleys' grass, and I caught the sweet scent of it as I rode past. The driveway was taken up by three cars, and other visitors would have arrived on foot. The move from Bruce's house to Marty's meant the compassionate ladies would have started all over again—cleaning, organizing, and bringing in fresh food. The potluck feast would continue until after the funeral, which was still two days away.

Sooner or later I'd have to bake my pineapple upside-down cake and carry it to Marty. That's what I always provide for a potluck. It's the only recipe I can count on, and besides, the bereaved do not appreciate experimentation. Comfort food must, by definition, be familiar and expected.

For the moment, I rode on past and continued my patrol. It was a relief to have an excuse for not facing Marty and the rest of the family.

All over town, life was moving on with the lazy, hypnotic rhythm of a porch swing. It was the kind of afternoon that makes me think of church revivals—stuffy and hot, with not much attention being paid.

I looked hard at people I met, wondering which of the men had attended the kegger in the woods. If

any of them glanced at me or spoke, I assumed a
stern posture, hoping to send the message *I know
who you are, and boy! are you in trouble!*

Several times I passed by Proctor's Gas Station,
and every time Billy Atwater was hard at work, as
if he didn't have a car stuck in the woods and alien
children to support. For a change he was out the
door at exactly closing time instead of lingering to
tinker with an engine. I watched him lock up, then I
made another pass through town and took Sundance back to the pasture.

Making my way through yards on foot, I returned
to the gas station by a ridiculously circuitous route
and let myself in through the open window at the
back of the garage. I'd told Mr. Proctor several
times he ought to lock that as well as the door, but
he'd never taken my advice.

Inside the garage, right by the car Billy had been
working on, were a couple of vending machines. I
dug a few quarters from my hip pack and purchased
dinner. Then I found a comfortable seat on a stack
of cast-off tires and waited.

Mayor Mooten had struck a chord with his campaign slogan and his inexhaustible attempts to
revive community spirit. There aren't many towns
where business owners leave windows open all
night, and damned few intruders would bother to
pay for their cheese crackers and grape Nehis.

For all my complaints to German about the
abnormally crime-free condition of our town, I worried about the complacency of its residents. If the
adult population had been tamed, the same could
not be said of our youth.

Most of the piddling misdemeanors on record could be laid at the feet of bored adolescents roaming loose and willing to take any opportunity to busy themselves for a few minutes. I worried that we were raising a bumper crop of full-fledged felons, and our calm and trusting citizens would be unprepared for the harvest.

In the few years I'd been out of school, I'd seen a tremendous change in the behavior of young people. Scott Carter isn't an unusual example, I thought, and mulled over a list of surly, ill-mannered teens I'd encountered lately.

What were parents doing in the good old days that they aren't doing now? I wondered.

Henry could be just what we need. A simple man, with determination and a vision. I'd have to try harder to support his efforts. From now on, I vowed, I'll be a regular at the potlucks, and the church socials, and if anybody throws a corn-shuckin', I'll put on my overalls and shuck ears till my fingers fall off.

Wouldn't it be nice if we could recapture the spirit and honesty and safety of that simpler time? I thought with a swelling of optimism. Then I remembered—it had really *been* that time when Lizzie Borden took an ax.

When it finally happened, it was so smooth and easy it might have been a well-rehearsed play.

I'd been dozing off and on in my steel-belted nest, letting night fall outside. I heard the sound of a body pushing itself through the window, saw the slender silhouette drop to the floor of the garage. I watched from my dark corner as he rifled through the carburetors and starters and transmissions littered on Billy Atwater's worktable, and I waited until he found the crankcase he was looking for, right beside the note that asked Billy to PLEASE FIX. Then I pulled my gun and stood up.

"You must be Jason," I said. "Let me introduce myself. I'm your match."

CHAPTER

12

I MARCHED HIM DOWN THE STREET TO THE PD, all the while wondering if I ought to worry about how often I'd pulled my gun lately. Jason was sullen and silent, but he made no effort to run for it. I read him his rights straight from the card, not daring to try it from memory and maybe forget a part. I wasn't about to take a chance on this case being thrown out of court on a technicality.

Bill's eyes were as big as saucers when I identified my prisoner. I had him frisk Jason, remove his wallet and the few odd items in his pockets, and Bill seemed almost honored to be allowed so close to the legend.

Naturally, I grabbed the wallet first thing and dug through it hungrily, scared to death I'd find out I'd actually arrested Mr. Proctor's night watchman or someone with equal embarrassment potential. The driver's license reassured me—the photo, while just as unflattering as any other, was a good enough likeness to guarantee that I'd arrested one Jason Baxter, a seventeen-year-old male, eyes and hair brown, of Antioch, Tennessee.

"So, Jason," I said. "Why did you choose Jesus Creek for your terrorist activities?"

He continued to stare at the wall, as unconcerned as if he were watching a mediocre movie.

"I gather you're exercising your right to remain silent," I said. "Care to call a lawyer?"

The only response was a grunt from Scott, who was watching the proceedings from his cell. I glared at him and reached to pat my gun, just in case Scott had forgotten I was the Bitch Cop with an Attitude.

"Okay, Jason," I said amiably, "let's just get you tucked in for the night. Hope you don't mind bunking with Scott. He talks tough, but he's a marshmallow inside. I'm sure the two of you will become fast friends. Heck, you may even become old friends before you're free again."

I was babbling and chuckling to myself, fairly bursting with excitement and the thrill of victory. The minute I had Jason safely behind bars, I allowed myself a hop step and a grin.

"Move over, Bill," I ordered. "I need the phone. Since young Jason is a minor, we'd best track down his parents and let them know their little boy is safe."

I knew that if I'd had eyes in the back of my head, I'd have seen Jason's face tighten. It's a common reaction. Every teen I'd ever encountered professionally was less concerned with the possibility of getting a criminal record than by having to face angry parents. Usually I felt sorry for the little felons, but not this time. I actually hoped to be present when Jason received a well-deserved parental thrashing.

In no time at all I had a name and phone number to match the address on Jason's driver's license. I savored every tone as I punched in the numbers, and forced myself to stop grinning. After all, it wouldn't do at all for me to giggle while delivering the news to the boy's unsuspecting parents that he was behind bars.

What thoughts must have been running through their heads all this time? I wondered. Jason had been on the loose in our town for well over a year. If, during that time, he hadn't called or otherwise communicated with his family, they'd probably given him up for dead. Wouldn't my news be the very miracle they'd prayed for? I thought, and felt a rush of pleasure. Every now and then I get to do a good deed, perform an act that pleases and delights, and those moments give me a sense of benevolent grace.

"Mrs. Baxter?" I asked of the woman who answered the phone. "This is Officer Kay Martin of the Jesus Creek Police Department. We have a young man here named Jason Baxter—"

"What?" she asked, even though she'd heard me well. "He's there? Is he hurt? Can I talk to him?"

"He's fine, ma'am, but I'm afraid he's in a little bit of trouble."

"Oh, thank God!" I could almost hear tears of relief rolling down her cheeks. "Thank God he's okay!"

In the background a man's voice asked for details.

"Oh, Bob," Mrs. Baxter said, "it's Jason! They've found him and he's okay! . . . Some police department. I didn't—"

I heard rustling as the phone was transferred

from hand to hand, then Bob himself came on the line.

"Who is this?" he demanded to know.

I repeated my name and the assurance that Jason was well and healthy. "Is the boy your son, Mr. Baxter?" I asked to clarify the relationship.

"Hell, no! He's no son of mine!"

Mrs. Baxter's startled cry of "Bob!" came through clearly.

"You keep him there, you hear?" Bob Baxter ordered. "Just keep the little shit locked up and don't call here again!"

I heard Mrs. Baxter protesting just before the connection was firmly severed. For a full minute I sat there with the dial tone buzzing in my ear while I tried to figure out what had just happened.

Bob Baxter was almost certainly Jason's father— "He's no son of mine!" generally means *Yes, he's my son and right now I'm so mad at him I could chew him up and spit him out*. In time, of course, those parents calm down and forgive whatever transgression has occurred.

I punched in the number again and waited through six rings before Bob answered.

"I told you to leave us alone!" he shouted. Mrs. Baxter was somewhere nearby, wailing at the top of her lungs.

"Mr. Baxter, if you hang up on me again, I'll have you arrested for . . . thwarting a criminal investigation in progress!" Quick thinking, wasn't it?

"What kind of investigation?" he asked. Then he remembered he didn't want to talk to me. "I've got nothing else to say!"

"Then put Mrs. Baxter on the phone," I ordered.

"She's already upset. I'm not going to have you making it any worse."

Still intoxicated with the power of the badge, I dropped my voice two notches. "Sir, if you persist in being difficult, I'll have both of you hauled in for questioning, and I'm sure that would be far more disturbing for the lady than a phone conversation."

In my mind I pictured him as a heavier, grayer version of Jason. I could imagine sullen resignation on his face and defiance in his stance as he realized I had the upper hand. Without another word, he passed the phone to the whimpering Mrs. Baxter, and I heard Bob's distant voice declaring, "Do whatever you want. I washed my hands of him a long time ago!"

"Hello?" the woman said tentatively. "Hello? Are you still there?"

"I'm here, ma'am," I assured her. "And I have a lot of questions. First of all, tell me how you're related to Jason."

"He's my son," she said tearfully. "My only son."

"I see. Now we've been aware of him here in this area for some time. When's the last time you heard from Jason?"

She didn't even have to think about it. "He left home a year and seven months ago. Jason and his dad had a head-on one night—you know how teenage boys will go out of their way to rebel against their parents. Well, Jason stormed out of the house and took off on that motorbike. He was fighting mad, and I was just scared to death he'd get himself killed, the way he was driving."

There was a pause in the conversation while she coped with a fresh burst of tears. I waited patiently through the sniffling and nose blowing before I tried another query.

"I gather your husband hasn't gotten over that argument," I said. "Do you mind telling me what it was about?"

Suddenly the talkative Mrs. Baxter turned shy. "You know," she said hesitantly. "Boys go through stages. They get these crazy ideas, and I just can't make Bob understand it'll pass."

"Please be more specific, ma'am." I had a pretty good idea where she was headed, but I didn't want to assume too much.

"Oh, you know." The sniffling continued, now aggravated by vague frustration.

"No, ma'am. I don't know. What, exactly, do you mean?"

She dropped her voice almost to a whisper. "It's just that Jason thinks he doesn't like girls. I told him and Bob both that the boy's just a late bloomer. So what if he's not interested in girls right now? But Jason got all upset, and before we knew it, he was going on about being . . . well, you know."

"Gay?" I prodded.

I assume she nodded into the phone.

"Mrs. Baxter," I said sternly, "are you aware that your son—your seventeen-year-old son—has been living in the woods through summer and freezing winter, alone, eating out of garbage cans . . . because of this?"

Fresh tears. "Bob told him he'd have to get out,"

she wailed. "He said Jason was sick and that he wasn't fit to live with decent people!"

"Well, ma'am," I said, with a heavy tinge of sarcasm, "I guess Jason believed him."

She had no response.

"We've checked with police departments all over, Mrs. Baxter," I added gently, because I felt bad about coming down so hard on that distraught woman for her husband's sins. "We'd have been in touch sooner, but we never found a missing teen report that fit what we had."

"Oh, that's not your fault," she assured me hastily. "Bob wouldn't let me go to the police. He didn't want anybody to know, you know."

Any sympathy that had lingered washed down the drain in a rush. "Are you telling me, ma'am, that your child has been missing for almost two years and you never reported that?"

"Well, I wanted to, but Bob said no." Now her sniffling had degenerated. She was whining, and I despise a whiner.

"Are you incapable of finding the police station on your own, Mrs. Baxter?" I asked acidly. "Do you not know how to dial a phone?"

She tried to interrupt with excuses and explanations but I was rolling and couldn't shut up.

"You think your son is sick, Mrs. Baxter? I'll tell you what's sick! Your husband's ignorant attitude and your pathetic desire to cater to his stupidity! That's sick, ma'am. And if I ever have children, I will do my best to remember you as an example of how not to be a mother!"

I slammed the receiver down so hard it would

probably never work again, then picked up a paper-weight just so I could throw something. All the while I was muttering obscenities that would have given Andrew Dice Clay a stroke.

When I spun my chair around to look for a heavier object to hurl, I saw Bill and Scott staring at me slack-jawed. Jason was standing with his face pressed against the bars, grinning at me.

"You've got a real nasty mouth," he said.

CHAPTER

13

FOR LACK OF A BETTER SOLUTION, I decided to leave Jason in lockup. He was a criminal, after all, I reminded myself. Why should I feel guilty? I would not fall in with the crowd and forgive his illegal acts simply because the boy had been disowned by his parents.

I'd have been content to spend the rest of the shift in the PD, but my restless stacking of papers and polishing of unsuspecting surfaces began to annoy Bill.

"Get out!" he ordered. "You won't find any crimes being committed in here. Go on now. Shoo!"

He didn't try this, naturally, until after I'd calmed down. It had taken a while, but once I'd vented all the anger I felt toward Jason's parents, I felt myself filled with lightness and purity, as if I'd been spiritually cleansed. I considered (briefly) the possibility of writing a self-help book—*Temper Tantrum Therapy*—but decided it wasn't weird enough or racy enough to get me on talk TV.

I'd called German at home to tell him about Jason's capture. He'd responded with a decidedly apathetic suggestion that I "write it up." After doing the bare minimum of paperwork, I'd called Mr. Proctor with explanation and apology for breaking into his place of business.

"You really ought to lock that window," I reminded him. "Next time it could be a burglar."

"Sure thing," he said. Exactly what he'd said every other time I'd made the suggestion.

With all the loose ends neatly tied up, I left the PD to continue my patrol. Once I got outside, the stillness of the night made me even antsier, but town was peaceful, and as usual, I couldn't find a single crime in progress. Jen had been returned to her family, the feds were launching a thorough investigation into the Brotherhood of Strength and their connection to the game warden's death, and Jason was behind bars. All was right with the world, except over at the Bradley house, where Marty's car sat alone in the driveway.

I couldn't believe that Bruce and Trina would have gone off and left him, but didn't dare leave it to chance. The least I could do was pop in for a quick visit. It was the neighborly thing to do.

Trina opened the door, looking exotic in her deep purple robe. "Come on in," she said, "if you don't mind the mess."

I looked around the almost sterile living room, wondering where one might find a mess in that house.

"We're in the kitchen, except for Bruce. He's only gone for milk, though, so he should be back any minute. Come have coffee—or food. Please, please have food." Her desperation was only half in jest.

The kitchen looked like a storage facility for a

caterer. Since my visit to Bruce's house, more cakes
and pies and hamburger casseroles had been delivered. There was a cooler on the floor to hold refrigerator overflow, and foil-wrapped items were in the
sink and covered with ice.

"Good grief!" I said. "I've never seen anything like
this."

"People are afraid I won't cook real food—meaning
meat-and-grease entrées—so they're making an extra
effort to bring it in." Trina poured coffee for me and
offered sugar and powdered creamer, which I
declined.

"They're doing it for Mere." Marty was seated at
the table, ignoring a plate full of tempting delights
on the table in front of him. "Everyone knew her.
They all have stories about jobs she did for them, or
little things she said or did."

"Isn't it odd?" Trina asked me. "We're heart-
broken, and going through the motions but all
caught up in grief. Then so many people come along
to help us, and we see that everybody is affected by
this. There's a little hole in each one of their lives
because Meredith isn't there to fill it anymore."

I hoped she wouldn't get carried away with the
wonder of friendship and forget to offer food again.
Those crackers I'd eaten at the gas station were
wearing off and the sight of fried chicken and potato
salad made my mouth water. Hunger, however, did
not override my sense of propriety.

"Meredith was a lovely woman," I assured them.
"We'll all miss her."

"I don't mean to blame you," Marty said, "but it's
made that much worse by having Vanessa in jail.

It's ridiculous that anybody could think she killed her own mother! There must be a way to make that clear."

My dinner slipped further away as I opted for honest tact instead of patronizing sympathy. "I know it's hard for you to believe, Marty, but the TBI has to operate on the evidence they have. There just doesn't seem to be another explanation."

"But we'll find one!" Trina added hastily. "We will, Marty."

I heard the front door open and close, then Bruce appeared in the kitchen doorway with a gallon of milk in his hand. "Kay! I didn't see your horse outside."

"I'm giving him the night off," I said. "Hoofing it by myself, you might say." I watched him shuffle the contents of the fridge in a valiant effort to find room for the milk.

No one else was amused. Eager to avoid returning to the subject of Vanessa's guilt, I tried a humble diversion. "We finally caught Jason. He's locked up at the PD right now."

They insisted on hearing every detail of the capture, and Trina pronounced me "dangerously clever." Then I told the rest of the story—how Jason had come to be a hermit in our woods, his parents' heartless rejection of him, and the way he'd grinned at me with a hint of appreciation in his eyes.

"Can you imagine?" Bruce asked, shaking his head. "Their only son, and they've cut him off because he didn't grow up to be the kid they ordered."

"Oh, but it happens all the time," Trina insisted.

"It does. Haven't you heard parents complaining about their daughter's hairstyle or their son's hobby? Or they'll shout out right in front of strangers or anybody, 'Junior, you eat like a pig! Sally, how could you be so stupid?' It's as if they're deliberately killing spirit."

"I know," I agreed. "Especially after talking to the Baxters. I've decided all our parents are out to get us."

"I've been luckier than most," Bruce said sadly.

Trina's eyes narrowed slightly and her mouth tensed. I wondered if she was remembering humiliation at the hands of her own family.

"Why do you suppose they do it?" I asked. "Surely they can see how it affects their children."

"Unfulfilled dreams," Trina said sharply. "And a sincere attempt to protect their children from the same mistakes they've made. A parent who always dreamed of being financially secure and never felt she'd reached that—even if there was plenty of money—will try to force a free-spirited child to work and scrimp and slave away at a sensible job instead of doing what he loves."

There was a flicker of recognition on Bruce's face, but it disappeared before Marty noticed. Trina, though, continued to watch her husband, unwilling to let him walk away from a fact he didn't seem inclined to deny.

"It's a shame all families aren't like this one," I said wistfully. "I can't get over the way you treat each other. I mean, Trina here could be a daughter instead of an in-law."

Marty's face turned bright red, as if it embarrassed him that I'd noticed his fondness for Trina. "I guess maybe I always did yearn for a baby girl," he said.

I remembered what Bruce had said about his own desire for a sibling of either gender and wondered if he'd ever discussed it with his father. Had it been only Meredith who'd decided a larger family was out of the question? Well, it should have been left up to her, my feminist brain declared. She'd have been the one to suffer through pregnancy and labor.

But wasn't teamwork the whole point of a family? I wondered. Didn't we band together in that particular way so that each of us could contribute our strengths and talents to benefit the group? Naturally, Meredith would have borne the burden of childbirth, but Marty would have shared the raising and expense of another child.

"And now you have two daughters," Trina said brightly. She took Marty's clenched fist in one hand and rubbed it gently with her other.

"It feels like I've lost one," Marty said. The blush had drained away, leaving his face gray and lifeless. "Vannie came here to get to know us, and it's caused her all this trouble. I doubt she'll care so much for this family now."

I heard Bruce's intake of breath and feared we were in for a communal cry. "I'm sure Vanessa won't blame any of you," I said carefully.

"There must be a way to prove to you, Kay, that Vannie didn't do this terrible thing." Trina was still holding her father-in-law's hand, but her intensity seemed to grab me by the shoulders. "If you go over

the evidence again. Look harder! I know you can
find the truth."

"I suppose I could take another look around the
shop," I said, helpless in the face of their faith.

It was hopeless, of course. The TBI would have
bagged and removed every speck of dust—but the
Bradleys were so buoyed by the possibility of a vital
discovery, I felt I had to try.

The door to the shop was closed, hiding the evidence and memories of Meredith's death. Marty
opened it for me and stood aside to let me enter first.
I switched on the light and looked around the room.
Inside the shop, the stale air held onto the odor of
decomposing flowers. Combined with the smell of
death, it was nearly enough to turn my stomach.

With Marty right on my heels, and Bruce and
Trina hovering in the doorway, I felt as if I were
under inspection. Looking around, hoping for inspi-
ration, I decided to start at the worktable where
Meredith had been when the killer attacked her. It
was bare now except for the residue left behind
after the TBI took prints. Not a single leaf remained
to give me hope.

To the left was Meredith's little card table/desk
and I scanned it quickly. It had been cleared of
every paper and pencil, but the computer and her
other tech-toys remained. I felt sure the TBI had
copied every file on the computer and were probably
wasting dozens of man-hours scouring the information, looking for a deathbed note typed by Meredith
as she collapsed.

The gritty powder from the print collection
covered every surface, and I didn't blame the

Compassionate Ladies for skipping this room; even if they'd have the guts for it, to have cleaned the shop would have been perceived as an excuse to pry, as unforgivable and indecent curiosity.

"I don't see anything unusual here. Do you?"

Marty peered over and around the desk and Bruce stepped in to take a look for himself. Feeling that I ought to do something, I stooped and looked at the underside of the desk. "There's something taped here," I said, amazed.

I was elated. The TBI had missed something, and I prayed real hard that it would turn out to be just the sort of evidence the Bradleys had hoped for. Pulling the small flashlight from my hip pack, I used it to illuminate the paper stuck to the underside of the desk.

"Can't see it from here. I'll have to crawl up under there." Dropping to my knees, I realized there wasn't enough room to get under the pint-sized desk that way.

I flopped over onto my back and tried to push myself along so that I could get a better look. When the handwritten note was still three inches ahead of my eye level, progress suddenly halted.

"Oh, for heaven's sake!" I muttered, and pushed myself back out into the open.

Trina had joined the men and all of them stood at my feet, radiating concern.

"What is it?" they asked in unison.

"I got stuck. Here." I sat up and removed the belt that held my hip pack, gun, and keys. "It may still be too narrow for my butt. If it is, Trina will have to crawl under there."

With the extra inches gone from my width, I started to try again, but the ringing of the telephone stopped me. We all stopped in our tracks, not sure whether we should waste time on answering it or continue what we'd started. By the time Trina said, "I'll get it," the machine had already picked up. The eerie sound of Meredith's voice on the taped message sent chills through me. It was a good quality recording, so lifelike . . . I sat straight up, bumping my head on the table in the process. Suppose it had been this machine Vanessa heard! It would be easy enough to think it was actually Meredith talking.

Trina stepped across my legs to the phone table and picked up the receiver, simultaneously shutting off the machine. She opted for "Hello" instead of "Flower shop."

She was trying to get rid of the caller quickly without being rude, and having little success. Meanwhile my attention had been captured by the little box beside the phone. I got to my knees and saw that it displayed Frankie Mae Weathers's home number. I understood why Trina couldn't bring the conversation to a close.

Could it have recorded the call that Vanessa mistook for a customer? I pushed the time button and saw the current date and time replace Frankie Mae's number. That was a feature I hadn't been aware of!

I pressed the review button, but instead of returning Frankie Mae's phone, it displayed OUT OF AREA. I pressed time again and saw that OUT OF AREA had called at 8:59 P.M.—a half hour before. The Caller ID was practically on my charge card, so taken was I with this dandy gadget. I went on pressing buttons and playing Name That Caller while Trina listened patiently to Frankie Mae's chatter.

When she was finally able to hang up, Trina's eyes were practically rolling in her head. "She means well . . ."

"But the road to hell is paved with Frankie Mae's intentions," I finished. "This gizmo is terrific. Look at this. It's a record of every call that's come in for . . . oh, I don't know. Several days. See?"

I pushed buttons, knowing the Bradleys had no interest in reviewing calls but so captivated I couldn't stop.

"Look, some nitwit tried to call you at six-thirty on Sunday morning!" I was appalled. Who would be so rude? I pressed on.

"Kay," Bruce said. "We'll give you the number box later if you'll just get back to work."

"Sure, Bruce," I said, barely listening. "Oops. It missed one. See? The call Marty made from the Tea Room isn't here."

I turned to ask if the Caller ID often failed to work, thinking that could influence my decision to purchase one. I saw Marty with my belt in one hand, my revolver in the other.

"I wanted to attend the funeral," he said morosely. "But it's just as well. Vanessa really ought to be there."

"Dad—" Bruce stepped toward his father, unconcerned about the gun.

"Bruce, you have to know I never would have let Vannie take the blame. I didn't even know she was going to be home that night! She was supposed to go straight from work to the Tea Room. I even thought of putting Mere in the cooler so it would seem she'd died much earlier, but I knew I'd have to make it easy to find her body when we got back here. Otherwise, she might have lain there for hours."

"We love you, Marty." Trina sounded as sincere as if she'd been talking to her newborn child.

Marty smiled. "And I love you kids. Vannie went straight to my heart, too, even if she did have so many of Mere's worst qualities. Blunt tongue, all work . . . you know how your mother was, son."

Bruce's eyes welled up with tears. "I know, Dad. But she always tried to do what was best for us."

"No, she didn't." Marty was firm on this point. "She did what she thought was best, and very often your mother was wrong. She bullied the rest of us until we gave in. Did you really want a business degree?"

"Well . . . but . . . it worked out. Now Trina and I can combine our skills—"

"I didn't want my father's lumber store, either," Marty said softly. "I wanted to be a musician, but that's not a steady income."

"You could've—" Bruce began.

"I tried. But Mere kept after me, and in spite of everything, I loved her. It wasn't so bad for me, but you, Bruce! I thought when you went to college, you'd break free. And along came this lovely girl"—he nodded toward Trina—"and I thought she could save you from your mother. But I came in here Saturday night, hoping to talk Mere into attending the opening. I tried to make her see you were happy

with Trina." He cast an apologetic glance at his
daughter-in-law. "Mere said the best thing for you
would be to get a divorce as fast as you could, and
that she'd see to it you didn't waste your life or your
future on Trina's scatty ways. I knew she'd do it,
too."

I was still on my knees, helpless to do anything
more than watch and listen as the Bradley family
crumbled. I could tell by Bruce's quick acceptance of
his father's words that he believed them. Neither
Bruce nor Marty doubted that Meredith had been
ruthless enough to destroy her son's marriage.

"Marty, listen to me." Trina took a stern tone with
him. "We can handle this, all of us together. We'll
find a way—"

"To get me off? No, you'll just waste every penny
of your inheritance, and in the end I'll still be a . . .
killer. To tell you the truth, I just don't think I've
ever had a backbone."

Marty pulled his son to him and hugged Bruce
until there was no breath left in either of them.
Then Marty walked to the cooler, opened the door,
and stepped inside.

We heard the sound of the door latching, and then
we heard a single gunshot.

CHAPTER

14

WAYNE AND I ATTENDED MARTY'S FUNERAL two days after Meredith's, along with our stunned neighbors. No one said it, or made any indication that they were thinking it, but I knew. I was to blame for Marty's death.

If I hadn't removed my gun to retrieve that scrap of paper, Marty Bradley would have carried on with his plan to confess as soon as he'd seen his wife properly buried. The final irony was that the paper hidden beneath Meredith's desk had been nothing more than her Christmas shopping list. As if to confirm what Marty had told us about his wife's plan for their son's future, Trina's name had been conspicuously absent from the gift items written there.

"Maybe you did him a favor," Wayne had said. He'd listened to my tearful version of events, alternately hugging me and handing me tissues, and he'd had the good sense not to deny my culpability. "The only other choice was prison, you know. Don't you think this way is easier for Marty? And for Bruce, too?"

He was probably right, but nothing could change or excuse the fact that my carelessness had given

Marty the opportunity to kill himself. "What if it isn't true?" I asked Wayne. "I think Marty must have tried to help Vanessa. He could've lied about that threatening phone call, you know."

"Could have. And you're pretty sure he left church that night to throw the brick, right?" Wayne reminded me of the only explanation we'd been able to imagine. "So he probably was trying to help Vanessa, but there's a big difference between those efforts and suicide. I'm sure Marty was telling you the truth, honey. There's at least some kind of justice here."

I wanted to believe he was right, but there would always be a question mark. Suppose Vanessa had killed Meredith . . .

Wayne nudged me out of my recurring reverie as the funeral service ended, and held my hand as we left the church with the other mourners.

We stepped through the wide oak doors and into the glaring summer sunlight. Most of those attending the funeral headed for their cars for the drive to the cemetery, but Wayne and I had decided to go straight home and burrow in for the day.

I noted flyers from the Brotherhood of Strength on car windshields and grimaced. A new sign in Eloise's window announced an upcoming fund-raiser to benefit the Landing Pad Project. Jen Atwater came out of the grocery store and gazed up at the sky as if she expected to see an old friend.

No matter how badly we're beaten, I thought, we manage to get up and move on. Already life in Jesus Creek was returning to normal.